ELOUISE EAST

Editor: Elouise East

Beta Readers: Courtney Green, Emma Brown, Cheryl Petit, Ash Knight, Autumn Sluder

❀ Created with Vellum

CONTENTS

DEFINITIONS — xi
LIST OF CHARACTERS — xiii

CHAPTER ONE — 1
CHAPTER TWO — 16
CHAPTER THREE — 29
CHAPTER FOUR — 43
CHAPTER FIVE — 60
CHAPTER SIX — 78
CHAPTER SEVEN — 90
CHAPTER EIGHT — 108
CHAPTER NINE — 131
CHAPTER TEN — 145
CHAPTER ELEVEN — 169
CHAPTER TWELVE — 182
CHAPTER THIRTEEN — 193
CHAPTER FOURTEEN — 211
CHAPTER FIFTEEN — 230
CHAPTER SIXTEEN — 246
CHAPTER SEVENTEEN — 259
FOUR MONTHS LATER — 277
FOURTEEN MONTHS LATER — 280
ONE YEAR LATER — 287
FOUR YEARS LATER — 300

About Elouise East — 303
Books by Elouise East — 305

INSTANT DESIRE

DEDICATION

To Courtney,
my partner in crime
my researcher
my sounding board
my confidant
my friend

DEFINITIONS

This is just a quick guide to help you understand some differences in childcare related jobs. This book is based in the United Kingdom so may have different definitions or job descriptions to your own country.

Babysitter—a person who cares for children for an evening or overnight, while parents go out. Usually for a very short time, i.e. a couple of hours.

Childminder—a person who uses their own home to care for children while parents are busy. Usually for up to twelve hours a day, and sometime overnight, several times a week.

Nanny—a person who goes to the parents' house to care for their children during the day, while the parents go to work.

LIST OF CHARACTERS
(ALPHABETICAL ORDER)

Analise, Bartender at Crush

Annie, Asher's sister, died two years ago

**Asher, Childminder, Sibling:
Annie, Niece: Janie**

Casey, Paramedic

Charlie, Bartender at Crush

Chloe, Paramedic

Clive, Owner of Thompson Architect
Company

Cooper, child Asher looks after

Dane, Zak's son

Darren, Sean's old teacher

Enrico, child Asher looks after,
Sarah's son

Ethan, Architect student, Sean's friend

Gemma, Server at Crush

Ginny, Tom's girlfriend

Janie, Asher's niece, under Asher's care when her mother died

Jocelyn, Trent's daughter, Babysits Janie

Laney, child Asher looks after, Sarah's daughter

Leo, child Asher looks after

Logan, Detective, Asher's friend

Martine, Asher's friend and fellow childminder

Max, Interior Designer, Sean's friend

Old Joe, Owner of Romano's

Owen, Gardener

Rosalia, Server at Romano's, Old Joe's daughter

Ryan, Lawyer, Martine's husband

Sarah, Enrico and Laney's mother

Sean, Architect, No surviving family

Tom, Manager of Crush, Ginny's boyfriend

Trent, Teacher, Asher's friend, Jocelyn's father

Zak, Woodworker, Sean's friend, Dane's father

CHAPTER ONE

ASHER

Asher felt the stares of other customers while he watched the children run after each other in the soft play centre, smiling softly as he heard them scream and shout in happiness. It was ear-splittingly loud, but the kids loved it there. He curled his hands around the coffee, letting his mind wander and allowed the prickling sensation of being watched to be pushed aside.

From the very beginning, being a male childminder in a predominantly female role was not easy—the stares, the comments, the whispers from people thinking they had a right to an opinion about his life. He was over it. After three years, it might come across as ignorance, but it was better than trying to defend himself. He'd tried that before, and it hadn't accomplished anything, so now, he just let the comments slide. He knew who his friends were and that was all that mattered.

"Asher! Sorry I'm late. The monkeys didn't want to cooperate this morning." Martine puffed up to the table with a double pushchair, moving chairs out of the way as needed, and parked it next to where he sat. Then she sat down hard and blew out a breath, swiping her hair off her neck. "Bloody hell, it's hot!"

Asher laughed. "You're the one who decides to walk everywhere, so you get no sympathy from me!" He stood up and leaned over to kiss her cheek. "I'll get you a drink. What would you like?"

"You're a gem. Something cold for now, thanks. You know the things I drink." Focusing on the pushchair, she started to unclick the straps, the children squirming to get free. "Sit still so I can reach the clips better!"

He snickered as he walked away, hearing her shout at the kids to take their shoes off before going to play. She never learnt. He always took their shoes off before letting the kids free, that way there was no having to chase after them. Asher shook his head, grabbing the fizzy drink she preferred and ordered another coffee to take back to the table. He gazed at her fondly as she struggled to get the kids sorted. Martine was a natural beauty, her dark brown skin flawless and perfectly complimented by her waist length jet-black hair. Her pouty lips, straight nose and big brown eyes were appreciated by many, including him. When they were out together, people often mistook them for a couple, but Martine had been married to Ryan for fifteen years now and had three kids to boot. Asher chuckled as he thought about her children. At thirteen, ten and seven, her boys were her life, but also her nightmare as she told it.

It was different for him. Being gay wouldn't have stopped him from becoming a parent if he'd wanted to, he knew that, he just hadn't wanted to so soon. Fate, unfortunately, had other ideas for him. Asher's sister, Annie, had died from breast cancer two years prior and, knowing it was coming, they had prepared his niece, Janie—as much as they could prepare a two-year-old—for the change in situation. Asher, understanding he was about to become guardian of a toddler, had resigned from teaching and began the process of becoming a childminder. He wanted to be at home with Janie to make it easier for them both to adjust. So, childminding had been the perfect solution for them.

"So, hotshot, have you decided to return to teaching when Janie starts school in September?" Martine threw the sentence at him before he'd even had a chance to sit down. She was never one to pull punches; she said what she thought regardless of the outcome. She took her drink and guzzled it down, before wiping her mouth with the back of her hand. "God, I needed that!"

Asher huffed a breath, second guessing his answer as he had done many times but knowing it was the right decision. He had been teaching primary school for almost three years before his sister's death. He enjoyed helping the children to understand whatever topic they were working on, developing new ways to get them thinking on their feet and, even, god forbid, the workload. Planning, organising and applying his knowledge made Asher feel like he was making his mark on the small part of the world they were in.

"No, I'm not going back." He glanced at Martine, whose eyes had widened comically. "I know I always said I would, but I like this job and the freedom it gives me and Janie. I can be there for her whenever she needs it, even if I have to bring several kids along with me." He laughed. "Actually, I've already decided to convert the garages."

"Wow! I never would have thought you'd be a lifer!" Martine's mouth twisted up in humour. "Welcome to the club."

"Very funny. Anyway, I've got an architect coming around to visit this afternoon to see what can be done." Asher drank his coffee, grimacing at the strength. He needed the caffeine though since Janie had woken after another nightmare last night. She hadn't had one for a while, but for the last two weeks, she had woken several times and Asher didn't understand why. He knew Annie's anniversary was coming up, but Janie wouldn't know that. Putting his mug down, he asked Martine for advice. "Janie's having nightmares again. I know we've been through them before, but I'm not sure what to do. I go to her or she comes to me, and we talk and hug it out. But I don't know what's caused it."

Martine placed her hand over his. "Just carry on what you're doing. There isn't much more you can do, unless you want her to speak to a psychologist again. Although, it wouldn't hurt to speak to them and see what they suggest. Didn't they say before the nightmares might come back?"

Asher nodded. "It has just been so long since the last one. I thought it was over for her. I hate seeing her like that." Every time he saw Janie with tears running down her fear-stricken face, it broke him.

"I know, Asher. It's not easy. She will get through them, and so will you." She squeezed his hand.

"Thanks." He sniffed back the tears threatening to fall and cleared his throat. "So, er, yeah, the architect is coming. I thought I would convert the garages into a self-contained childminding unit. Make it separate from the house. What do you think?"

Martine allowed the change of subject with a pat of his hand. "I think it's a really good idea, as long as you're definitely staying with childminding. No point if you're going to change your mind later."

"No, I've decided. It's just a better fit."

"In that case, spill. Tell me what you want it to look like." Martine leaned forward on her elbows, head resting on her fist.

Asher laughed. "Always hungry for gossip, aren't you? Well, I want there to be a small kitchen so we can make lunch and do baking and things like that. There obviously needs to be a toilet, but I was wondering whether to put a shower in there too, in case of emergency situations!" Asher gave her a knowing look.

Martine coughed up the drink she had just taken, laughing. "That is actually a very good idea." She cocked her head. "And one I might take on board too."

"The rest, really, I think of as open space that can have storage added to it, as well as tables and chairs. I think the space would be big enough to fit what I would need for the little ones and have a sofa and TV for the after schoolers if they want it. It would still need access to the garden, but the door that's already there should only need replacing with a more secure one." Asher was excited about the prospect of it all. He had saved enough money over the past few years to be able to afford the conversion without a loan. It would mean a heavy dent in his savings, but what he and Janie would gain from it would be money well spent.

"Sounds good. Are you fitting it out with completely new furniture or using what you already have?" Martine swooped forward to pick up one of the kids, resting him on her knee. Grabbing a tissue, she wiped the boy's nose, tickling him when he squirmed. "I have some stuff at mine that I'm not using anymore, especially storage. You're welcome to come and root through. Ryan will definitely appreciate you taking it off our hands." She set the boy on his feet, ruffling his hair before he ran back off to play.

"Thanks, I might just do that. I'll wait until after I've spoken with this guy first, so I have an idea of what's possible and what's not." Asher took a drink of his now cold coffee, grimacing when he realised it tasted much stronger.

"What company is coming around?"

He frowned, thinking. "Thompson Architect Company, I think. I remember the guy's name is Sean Edwards. He's supposed to visit about one."

Leaning forward again, Martine reached for her purse. Standing, she winked, "Well, I expect a phone call to hear details of how hot he is." With that parting note, she smirked then walked to the counter, ignoring his grumbled remarks about not being interested in any guy at the moment.

While Martine was ordering lunch, Asher went to the ropes of the soft play. "Janie! Enrico! Laney! Come to the table, please!" He picked up the lunch menu, perusing what he thought they would like. Knowing them, it would be chicken nuggets and chips, and surely enough, when the kids came running, they each chose what Asher thought they would. "Okay, kiddo's, have a drink then go back and play. I'll shout you again when it's ready." Each child obligingly drank, albeit a small amount, then ran off, shouting for each other.

He adored those kids. Naturally, Janie held a special place in his heart, but he loved all the children he cared for. Three times a week, he had Enrico and Laney, who were siblings, and on the other two days, he looked after Leo and Cooper. He was very lucky to have such good kids and parents. Many a time he heard horror stories, mainly from Martine, of parents who treated their childminders like a piece of dirt, and Asher was so glad he'd never had that happen. At least, not yet.

After Martine had returned, Asher took her place and ordered lunch for him and the kids, refilling his coffee again. He rubbed his hands against his gritty, tired eyes, feeling the pressure behind them, which signalled a headache on the horizon. Blowing out a breath, he paid for his order and tried to concentrate on his conversation with Martine.

Consuming lunch had taken up a considerable amount of time and patience because the children kept wanting to go and play instead of eating. With Asher's persistence, they each cleared their plates and drank more, then he took them all for a toilet break. Janie and Enrico were both independent, but Laney was still in nappies, and once everyone was sorted, Asher's headache was a dull throb in his forehead.

Arriving back at the table, Asher looked at Martine. "I'm going to have to go, Mar, my head is killing me." He began to pack up the things he'd brought with him, asking the children to try and put their shoes on.

"Okay, Asher, make sure you get some painkillers when you get home, all right?" Martine squinted at him, after glancing briefly at Janie. "And contact the you-know-who about the dreams. They may have more advice for you."

Asher peered at Janie to see if she had heard what they were talking about, but she was too busy helping Laney with her shoes. He nodded. "I will, but maybe tomorrow. I think if I do much more today, my head will explode. I still have this meeting to get through." He rolled his head on his neck to try and loosen some of the tension. "Come on, gang."

The kids jumped up and ran to hug Martine. Circling the table, Asher followed suit. "I'll speak to you later."

She called after him, "You better. I want all the details!"

He sent a wave over his shoulder as he held Laney's hand to exit the building. "Janie, Enrico, make sure you stay with me while we walk to the car, please." He trusted them both to listen as he had taught them to, and they safely arrived at the car. After buckling them all in, Asher sat himself in the driver's seat and massaged his forehead before heading for home. He had a couple of hours before he had to do the school run, and maybe, just maybe, these three might take a short nap for him. *I can wish, can't I?* He shook his head and huffed out a breath. *Yeah, that won't happen.*

SEAN

The Thompson Architect Company, or TAC as the employees called it, had a good reputation for being fair, inexpensive and for completing good work. And for as long as Sean had been involved with the company, he had never seen otherwise.

Sean had spent his three years of mandatory university work experience working for TAC and learning how the architectural business worked, and when he had graduated last year, they had offered him a full-time position straight away. He'd been one of the lucky ones, and he'd known it, so had grabbed the opportunity with both hands.

Money was not the driving factor for that choice. He would never want for money again since the insurance payout had arrived four years ago. Although he hadn't wanted to touch the money at first, he'd been talked into using it. He knew, deep down, his parents would have wanted him to use it to help his career; it had just been difficult, knowing where it came from. He had no siblings so, when his parents had died after their car was hit by a drunk driver, he was left alone. Neither of his parents had siblings, Sean's grandparents had already passed, and there was no other extended family.

So, Sean had paid off his tuition fees, bought a house and a car, and invested the rest. He was glad he had now, he was free and clear of debt and had the stability to do whatever he desired. And being an architect was all he'd ever dreamed of. At primary school, he had entered any building or drawing competitions they had, he created models for his homework whenever he could, and he studied other architect's work in his spare time. This carried on through secondary school as well, driving his tutors crazy with the amount of work he often presented.

He found a kindred spirit in his design and technology tutor, and they were often found talking about the intricacies of ergonomics and sustainability. That same tutor helped him choose the right course for him to continue with, and the rest, as they say, was history.

He'd not been in contact with Darren—as his tutor had told Sean to call him when he had left school—for a while, he couldn't actually remember whether he had called him since his parents had died. He would have to remedy that soon.

Sean checked his watch after he'd parked the car, noticing he was early, as usual. He hated being late, so he always ended up waiting around for the correct time before heading to his appointment. *Better early than late*, his father always said. But he sometimes wondered how much of his time was spent waiting around.

He pulled out the folder containing the information on his next client, and even though he had it memorised, he flicked through it again. Asher Danvers wanted a two-car garage conversion into a secured self-contained unit with access to the garden area. It seemed simple enough, but Sean would have to wait and see what Mr Danvers said in person. Sean had realised early on in this job that what information was passed on over the phone, was not always everything the client had on their mind.

Eyeing his watch again, he blew out a breath. He had another five minutes before he could go without appearing to be ridiculously early for the appointment. Max had always laughed about this quirk of his, but that was because Max was always late.

Sean had met Max Hughes, by chance, at a bar in Sean's sixth year of architecture and Max's first year of interior design. They were both attending different universities in Cambridge and had been trying to gain the bartender's attention. They'd ended up in conversation, then decided to join their respective parties together for a huge night out.

So, when Sean had accepted the offer at TAC, he had come armed with knowledge of an interior designer, who he had incorporated into some of his jobs as soon as Max had qualified. Max was grateful, and his business had boomed with the referrals he'd received from Sean. They were a good team.

Sean checked his watch once more and smiled, three minutes early exactly. He climbed out of the car, holding tight to the folder as he shut the door and headed to Mr Danvers' front door. He could see the two garages that Mr Danvers wanted converted, and they looked in reasonable condition, but Sean would withhold judgement until he saw the inside—that was where many properties let their owners down.

Walking past the neatly kept garden to the front door, Sean knocked. He gazed around as he waited for an answer, which when it came, heralded a figure he had not expected.

Mr Danvers was no older man wanting to make a live-in unit for his family to visit, which is what Sean had envisaged. No, Mr Danvers was a gorgeous, six-foot, brown-haired, golden-eyed wonder with scruff that looked like it would feel amazing on Sean's skin.

Sean was startled from his musings with that thought and quickly held out his hand. "Mr Danvers? I'm Sean Edwards from Thompson Architect Company." He cleared his throat as he waited for the guy to welcome him.

"Ah, yes, hello." He shook Sean's hand. "Please, call me Asher."

They stood facing each other for a moment before a loud crash, silence, then a screaming cry sounded from within. Sean jumped as Asher spun around and raced down the hallway Sean could see from the front door.

Sean wasn't quite sure what to do. He'd not been invited in, but he didn't want to stand here and leave the door open. He decided to step inside and shut the door behind him. Waiting in the large entryway, Sean studied his surroundings briefly—stairs to the right side and dark wood flooring as far as the eye could see. He could see the open plan living room through an archway to the left and a similarly presented dining room to the right. Straight ahead, he saw another door.

He heard talking from further inside, so he decided to follow the sound, making sure his footsteps were heard as he approached what he thought was the kitchen.

Entering the kitchen, his assumption being correct, he saw that Asher was on his knees cradling a child in his arms as he talked in soft tones. Asher peered up at him, and Sean saw panic in his eyes.

"Could you get me some ice, please?" Sean saw

Asher indicate the freezer on the other side of the kitchen. He paused, then went over to do as asked. Finding an ice pack, he looked around for a towel and wrapped it up before handing it to Asher.

"Is he all right?" Sean asked.

CHAPTER TWO

ASHER

Asher had never felt fear like he had when he'd heard that scream—it was a completely different type of fear than when he was watching his sister die. That was a slow burning fear of unfairness, whereas this was unmitigated "holy shit" fear.

He'd known exactly who it was when he'd started running through the house—Enrico—the boy who could cause trouble by just standing still in the middle of an open space. Asher had known something was seriously wrong though, he had never heard that sound come out of Enrico's mouth in the two years he'd cared for him.

Holding Enrico in his arms now, the fear was dialling down a little but the bump on Enrico's head was enormous. He hadn't wanted to leave him to fetch the ice pack though, so he was glad when this Sean guy had entered the kitchen and responded to Asher's request without complaint.

Repositioning the ice pack on Enrico's forehead, Asher noticed he was looking very pale. His first aid training was whirling through his head, but his instincts were telling him Enrico needed the hospital. It had only taken a few seconds for him to get to Enrico, but he was unsure if Enrico had lost consciousness or not. Asher always followed his instincts, so he asked for help from a stranger, yet again.

"Sean, could you pass my mobile from the table, please?" Asher glanced toward Sean, seeing him already in motion as if he needed something to do. When Sean went to pass it to him, Asher asked, "Could you ring through to his parents for me? I'll talk to them but if you can dial and hold the phone?"

"Um, sure, okay." Sean flipped the phone around so he could use it. "Um, it has a passcode."

"Oh, yeah, 3498. And if you can go into contacts and find the number for Sarah Romano work." Asher repositioned the ice pack again, checking Enrico's breathing, which seemed normal, and his pulse, which was a little fast. He glanced over at Laney, checking to make sure she wasn't panicking about Enrico, but she looked fine playing with her baby and pushchair.

Sean placed the phone in front of Asher as the phone began to dial. He hoped he wouldn't have to leave a message.

"Hey, Asher, everything okay?" Sarah's voice sounded worried as Asher expected it to. He had never rung her before when he was looking after Enrico and Laney, he only ever sent text messages or photos.

"Hi, Sarah. Enrico has had a fall off the kitchen chair. He has a nasty bump to his forehead and, although his breathing and pulse seem fine, I would feel better having the hospital check him over." Asher hoped he sounded calm; he didn't want to worry her any more than necessary.

He heard Sarah blow out a breath on the other end of the phone. "Okay, um, I can come get him and take him. I'll come now. Is he okay?"

"Sarah, he's okay, it's just a bump. I'm being overly cautious, all right? I can take him to the hospital if you like and you can always meet us there?" Asher would have gone with them anyway, even if he hadn't offered to take Enrico himself, and it made more sense as Sarah was already closer than he was.

"Are you sure, Ash?"

"Absolutely. I'll head over now."

"Okay, thanks Asher. I'll be there as soon as I can." Sarah hung up.

"Right, Enrico, let's get you sorted so we can go on a road trip, eh?" Asher removed the ice pack and tried to keep his voice upbeat and cheerful so as not to worry either child. As he scanned around, he realised he couldn't see Janie. "Janie?" He knew she didn't like it when anyone got hurt, she was usually trying to make them better. She would make a great doctor one day.

He noticed Sean stand up and walk to the lounge doorway. Sean peered back at him and indicated into the room with the hand still holding Asher's phone.

Asher lifted Enrico in his arms and went through to the lounge with Laney trailing behind and noticed Janie sat on the sofa with Albert in her arms—she went everywhere with that bunny, a gift from her mother. He sat Enrico on the sofa next to Janie, taking in her tear-stained face.

"You okay, sweetheart?" Asher rested his hand on Janie's knee as he crouched, trying to look in her eyes.

Janie nodded and clutched her bunny tighter, sniffing.

"All right then." Asher knew Janie would talk to him when she was ready, if not, he would push later when there were no kids around. "Well, we're going to go on a road trip to see a doctor. We might get to see some ambulances, too."

Asher stood upright, reaching for the changing bag of items he took everywhere with him and checked quickly through to make sure he had the essentials.

"Ambances!" Laney shouted, excitedly. "Ambances!"

Asher laughed as he hooked the bag over his shoulder. "Yes, Laney, ambulances. Right kids, let's go jump in the car." He had completely forgotten about Sean until he turned to head to the front door and saw him standing there awkwardly.

"God, sorry, Sean. Can we rearrange for another day, please?" Asher grabbed hold of Laney's hand and used his other to steady Enrico as they exited the house.

"Um, sure." Asher saw Sean following them to the car. "Do you need any help?"

"Don't worry, I'll be fine," Asher said, although he really didn't feel fine. He was mortified that Enrico was hurt, and his hands were shaking, but he was on autopilot now. "Thank you for your help in there." Asher unlocked the car and pulled open the passenger side so Laney and Janie could climb in.

Asher glanced toward Enrico, noticing he looked even paler in the sunlight. "How are you doing, Enrico?" he asked, calmly.

Enrico gazed at him with worryingly glazed eyes but nodded his head, wincing as he did. Asher helped Enrico get into the car seat, and then strapped him in. He rushed around the other side to buckle the other two in and placed the bag on the floor.

Closing the passenger doors, he took a deep breath and closed his eyes for a moment. It always felt worse to him when it was the children he looked after that got hurt. It was horrible regardless of who it happened to, but when someone was paying you to take care of their child, and then that child gets hurt, it makes everything feel ten times as bad.

Walking around to the driver's door, he saw Sean standing there waiting for him, holding out his phone.

"Give me the keys," Sean said, holding out his other hand.

"Sorry?" Asher had no idea what he was talking about.

"Let me have the keys. I don't think you're in any state to drive right now. I'll drive you." Asher stared at Sean dumbfounded. Why would he do this? "It's no big deal, Asher. Let me help. I know you don't know me from Adam but let me help."

Asher felt a weight lifted from his shoulders and held out the keys, taking his phone back. As their fingers touched, a spark of electricity flicked down Asher's arm, and his eyes shot to Sean's, seeing his flash wide. Sean snatched his hand away, turning to the house.

"Where are you going?" Asher called to him.

Without turning back, Sean called over his shoulder, "To lock your front door," which he proceeded to do, then returned to the vehicle, sitting behind the wheel.

Asher wasn't sure how he felt about Sean driving his car, but the one thing he did know was that he was grateful at that moment. He rested his head back as Sean reversed out of the driveway, pointed the car towards the hospital and began the short drive in silence.

SEAN

Driving this huge family car was a bit of a culture shock for Sean—he had never been in one of these as a passenger, and now here he was, driving one. He was just grateful that cars were pretty much the same, otherwise it would have been a bit embarrassing.

Sean didn't even know why he'd offered; it had just come out of his mouth when he saw how wrecked Asher had looked as he walked around the car towards him. He certainly hadn't had any intention of heading towards a place which held such bad memories; he hadn't visited a hospital since his parents had died.

Sean hoped he would be able to drop them off at the entrance, park Asher's car, and then get a taxi back to his own car.

He was distracted by Asher, maybe that was why Sean was acting strange. Heading towards the appointment earlier, Sean had expectations, which hadn't been correct; it had thrown him for a loop, and he had never recovered.

In the small confines of the car, Sean was able to admit Asher was good looking—and smelt amazing—

but that was it, he wouldn't allow his thoughts to go anywhere else.

Sean cleared his throat. "How's he doing?"

Asher flinched, probably at hearing Sean's voice after so much silence, then glanced to the back seat again. "He's awake but staring out the window. The goose egg on his head looks awful though," he replied. Out the corner of his eye, Sean saw Asher rub his hands over his face. "Thanks again for this. I could have managed, but you've made it so much easier. I appreciate it."

"Not a problem." And it wasn't, although Sean made a mental note to call the office and reschedule his next appointment, he wasn't going to make it to Peterborough by four. "I'm sure he'll be fine." Sean wasn't a doctor, but it seemed polite to try and offer some comfort.

They lapsed into silence again as they approached the hospital. Asher directed Sean to where they needed to be, and he tried to hide how uncomfortable he was by keeping quiet. He parked the car and got out to help Asher get his things together.

He watched Asher firmly place the backpack on his shoulders before unstrapping the two girls. "Both of you hold onto my hand, please," Asher told them as he walked them round to the other side for Enrico. "Now, you know the drill, stand by the wheel and put your hand on the circles." Both girls obediently did as he asked—Sean noticed there were handprint circles on the side of the car—and Asher unstrapped Enrico, lifting him into his arms and getting him situated before turning to the girls and holding his hand out again. They grabbed his fingers and, without waiting, they all began to walk towards the entrance.

Sean dallied for a moment before his conscience got the better of him. He ran after Asher and his troupe. "Hey, wait up!" Asher turned to watch over his shoulder. When Sean got to him, he reached for Enrico. "Let me take him. You might need to fill out forms or something."

Asher hesitated briefly, then acquiesced, letting Sean carry Enrico the rest of the way to the doors. Sean beat back the panic as they got closer to their destination. He repositioned the boy, who had rested his head on Sean's shoulder, and clutched him a little tighter.

They all entered the hospital and headed for the reception desk. Sean trailed behind Asher but kept him within reach, he didn't want anything else to happen to the kid.

He distantly heard Asher begin to talk to the nurse as he inspected the almost too-familiar area. Even though he had not set foot in this hospital for four years, nothing much had changed. It had been updated a bit, worn out chairs replaced with new ones, same with the displays but for the most part everything was the same. The feeling of nausea crashed over him, and he began to breathe deeply to stave it off.

"Sean?" He flicked his glance to Asher when he heard his name. "We can go sit down. Do you want me to take him?"

It took a few seconds for the words to register and the fog of nausea to recede from his body. "Oh, um, no, it's okay. I got him." Sean began walking to the uncomfortable looking chairs and sat down with Enrico on his knee.

He couldn't believe he was sat in a hospital waiting area after he had sworn he would never again.

"—you okay?" Sean realised Asher was talking to him again and tried to clear the memories from his brain.

"Yeah, sorry, don't have the best memories of hospitals." Sean couldn't believe that had just come out of his mouth—he hadn't meant to say anything.

"Oh god, I'm sorry, do you want to go?"

Yes, he thought, but his mouth had other ideas. "No, I'll be okay. Did they say how long the wait was?" Enrico had snuggled himself right into Sean's body, calming him.

"Not specifically, only that it shouldn't be long. I'm hoping Sarah can get here before he has to go through. It will be a bit awkward taking all three of them in." Asher set the backpack on the floor and kept his eyes on the two girls who were playing nearby with the toys. "She should be here soon though."

"I could watch after them if you want?" Sean had no idea what was wrong with him today, he didn't know the first thing about children. His friend Zak had not long had a baby boy, but that didn't mean Sean was able to look after him.

"That would've been helpful but, unfortunately, I can't let you. Legally, I mean. Because I look after Enrico and Laney as a business, I have to have the correct documents and everything before I can leave them with someone else." Asher looked apologetic. "Thank you for the offer though."

"That's okay, I understand." With that statement, Sean felt Enrico sit more upright.

"Enrico, sweetie, you okay?" A woman, he could only presume was Enrico's mum, crouched down in front of them, briefly glancing at Sean before focusing on her son again. She raised a hand to Enrico's face and gave a small smile. "Oh dear, that's going to leave a mark, isn't it, sweetheart!" Enrico made no move to get off Sean's knee, so he didn't force him to. He was sure his mum would take him when she was ready.

"Sarah, I'm so sorry about this. It all just got—" Asher began to talk but got enveloped in a hug from Sarah.

"Don't be silly, Asher. It was an accident. Don't worry about it." Sarah palmed Asher's face, giving him a gentle pat, and Sean could see she was definitely a mother.

"Mummy!" Sarah got attacked from behind by her daughter, and she laughed.

"Hey, sugarplum. You okay?" Sarah turned and got down to Laney's level.

"Enrico got hurt, Mummy, we comed here to see ambances! I not see them. Where are ambances, Mummy?"

Sarah laughed at Laney's long speech and quickly told her that the ambulances were probably busy, but they might get to see some later. Laney, having been reassured, ran back to play with Janie.

Sean kept quiet throughout the exchanges, not wanting to interrupt, until Sarah turned to him, a question in her eyes.

"Hi, I'm Sean." Sean held out his hand for her to shake. "I'm just along for the ride. I had an appointment with Asher." Sean winced when his words didn't come out quite right.

"Sarah, remember I told you I was getting an architect to come around to talk about the conversion?" Asher waited for Sarah to nod. "This is the architect."

Sarah nodded, understanding lighting her eyes.

"Enrico Romano?" A nurse called the boy's name. Sarah put her hand up briefly before bending to take Enrico off Sean's knee.

"Thank you," Sarah said as she turned. "Asher would you mind keeping Laney with you for a few minutes, please?"

"Sure thing." Asher nodded.

"Laney, sweetie? I'm just taking Enrico to see the nurse. I'll be back in a minute, okay?"

"Okay, Mummy," Laney answered as she continued playing with the dollhouse with Janie.

Sarah rolled her eyes at them, smiling, then carried on walking to where the nurse was waiting.

Asher dropped himself into the chair beside Sean, leaning forward to rest his arms on his thighs. He rubbed at his face briefly, then lifted his head to watch the two girls. Sean noticed he did that often. He understood that it was Asher's job, but he seemed hyper-aware of the children he looked after. Maybe it was because of what happened, Sean didn't know.

"Are you okay?" Sean ventured.

Asher nodded slowly. "Yeah, just annoyed at myself for letting this happen."

Without thought, Sean reached a hand to Asher's back and rubbed along his spine. "It wasn't your fault." Realising what he'd done, he apologised and removed his hand.

CHAPTER THREE

ASHER

Asher's body almost followed Sean as he moved his hand away, but he caught himself in time. To cover, he blurted out the first thing that came to mind, "God, I hate hospitals too." Then he winced and glanced at Janie to see if she'd heard—he didn't want her scared of hospitals. Satisfied she hadn't, he peered at Sean and gave him a crooked smile. Lowering his voice, "My sister died three years ago from cancer. If I had never visited one again, I would've been happy."

"I'm so sorry, Asher. Shit." It was Sean's turn to wince, checking the kids weren't listening to his words.

"Thanks." He sat upright, shaking his head. "I don't know why I even said that. Sorry. Ignore me. I'm sure you have other things to do than sit here and wait with us, especially when you don't like being here in the first place." He watched Sean for any indication he was going to run but seeing none.

Sean studied his hands, a wry smile on his face. "My parents died in a car accident four years ago. This was the last place I saw them," he said quietly.

Asher lifted his hand and rested it on Sean's shoulder, squeezing slightly. "I'm sorry for your loss. It's never easy losing someone close to you." Asher gazed at Janie playing alongside Laney. From the outside, no one would be the wiser that this little girl had lost her mother when she was two years old and had been given to Asher for safe keeping.

Realising he still had his hand on Sean, he removed it after a final squeeze in commiseration. Clearing his throat and changing the subject, he asked, "How long have you been an architect?"

Asher saw Sean sit straighter. "About a year. I got hired on by TAC as soon as I'd finished my degree— I'd done my work experience there, so we both knew what we were getting out of it, which was good."

"TAC?" asked Asher.

"Oh, sorry. Thompson Architect Company. We call it TAC."

"Ah, I would ask if you enjoy it, but I can see that you do." Asher could see a spark flicker in Sean's eyes that had been missing during the previous parts of their conversation. He was visibly more content.

"Yes, I do. It's what I've always wanted to do and

have worked hard to get where I am." Sean didn't seem defensive about his answer, just stated a fact.

"I'm sure you did. Is there any part you like better than others?" Asher was trying to keep the spark alive; he was certain if the conversation changed subject, it would die out again. He wished he knew why, though he suspected it had something to do with Sean's parents.

"Wow, um, the actual designing is great. Although the main ideas are the clients, I get to create something from that. I take their ideas and take the limitations of the area they're wanting to redesign, and then create something new." Sean used his hands to emphasise his words.

"I never thought of it like that before." Asher was impressed that Sean knew what he wanted from life and had gone for it. Yes, Asher had become a teacher, but it had been his second choice. His first was to be a photographer. It was his mother that had persuaded him to change his career to something she thought would be more secure. He understood why, and that's why he'd agreed.

"It has its ups and downs, though, like any job, I suppose." Sean chuckled. "I hate the admin side of things. It drives me crazy!"

Asher laughed. "I can imagine. I'm in a similar situation. I enjoy working with the children, but the paperwork kicks my ass every time. Same for when I was a teacher. I think most people are in the same boat —they enjoy the physical side of their job, but the paperwork is a necessary evil."

"Definitely." Sean repositioned himself on the chair. "So, what is it you want to do with your garage?" Asher glanced over at him and saw he was watching Asher, smiling. "We may as well discuss it while we're here."

Asher eyed his watch, noting they had only been there for forty-five minutes—it had seemed like a lot longer. Settling back in his seat, he crossed his arms and stretched his legs out in front. Eyes on the kids, he tried to explain what he wanted. "So, I basically want to separate my childminding business from the main house, making it completely self-contained—its own kitchen, shower room, toilet and an open space for playing and a sofa."

Asher was excited about the prospect of being able to separate his home life from his work life. He had heard many childminders say they wished they could separate the two sides. He was hoping it would become reality for him.

It wasn't that he didn't have enough space to have both in his house—he did—but he wanted to give Janie somewhere she could decompress, just like Asher needed to.

"Okay, that sounds doable." Sean nodded his head, eyes down as if in thought. "The information I have says you want to keep access to the garden. What about the garage doors and any windows? What do you see for them?"

"I'd like to have a separate entrance so parents wouldn't have to come down the side of the house to get through to the garage. And I'd like to see who is at the door so some windows would be nice, letting in some extra natural light as well. I'm not bothered about the garage doors, to be honest. I'm happy for them to stay if it would work better as long as they could be boarded off or something on the inside."

"I think we may be better taking the doors out and bricking it up with some windows added. Which side does the sun come in?"

Asher wondered where Sean was keeping all this information or whether he would have to go through it with him again later. "As you're facing the house, it comes up on the right of it and works its way across the front."

Sean nodded. "Okay, so some windows on the side and front of the garage would be handy."

Asher cocked his head at Sean and couldn't stop his curiosity. "Where are you putting all this info? You're not writing anything down."

He saw Sean smile. "I have a very good memory. I'll remember it, don't worry."

"I wish my memory was as good—it must be my old age." Asher chuckled to himself. He was trying to figure out how old Sean was—he didn't know how long an architecture degree was so that was not helping but he guessed mid-twenties.

Sean laughed. "You're not that old." Asher saw a blush darken Sean's face.

"Why, thank you, kind sir." Asher enjoyed Sean's blushes more than he should. He wanted to see more of them. Asher shook his head to try and get rid of the thought, but it wouldn't go. Sean was gorgeous with his sandy-brown coloured hair combed back against his head and his bright blue eyes. He had an air of innocence around him if you missed the look of pain in those eyes. Sean already had laughter lines around his mouth, which made Asher think he must be fun to be around. And a goddamn dimple, sneaking in on his right cheek. Asher couldn't see much of his other side so didn't know if there was one there too.

"Asher?" A voice interrupted his musings, although toned with a question that made him think it wasn't the first time his name had been said. He turned toward the voice, seeing Sarah there holding Enrico's hand. He stood and went to them.

"Hey, how's he doing?"

Sarah peered down at Enrico and smiled. "He's absolutely fine. The doctor checked him over, and apart from checking on him every two hours through the night, they said he should make a full recovery in a few days." Laney raced over to her mum.

"I'm glad. I'm so sorry, Sarah," Asher began.

"Stop. It was an accident, that's all. You did everything you should have done. He'll be fine." Sarah was forceful with her words. She knew him well enough to know he'd be beating himself up about this for a while. "Let's head home, kids. Asher, I'll take Laney with me, too, saves me coming back again later. I'll keep you up to date. But stop worrying. Enrico is fine."

"Okay, thanks. And yes, please, let me know how he is. I'll need you to come and sign an accident form at some point."

"Sure, no problem. Well, come on then, kids. Let's go."

"Let me just get Laney's things for you." Asher went to his bag and got out a spare carrier bag and filled it with Laney's things, then brought it back over to Sarah.

She rested her hand on Asher's forearm. "Stop, Asher. Please. He's fine."

Asher nodded, staring at the floor. Clearing his throat, he said goodbye and watched them exit the hospital. Blowing out a breath, he turned for Janie and remembered Sean was still there too. He raised his eyebrows when he saw Janie sat next to Sean, pointing to things in a book she held on her lap, and Sean leaning closer to her, watching and talking.

His heart skipped a beat when they both laughed. They made such a sight that Asher found it hard to breathe for a minute. Then he closed his eyes, took a deep breath and headed towards them.

"Hey, Janie. Are you looking after our guest?"

"I'm reading the book to him. We're going on an adventure." Asher had been surprised when Janie had taken to reading despite her age. She could read almost any child's book, and she hadn't even started primary school yet. She was very bright for her age, he'd been told.

"That sounds great. We must go now though, sweetheart. Can you put the book back for me, please?" Asher grabbed his backpack as Janie did as he asked and glanced towards Sean. "We'll get you back to your car shortly."

Sean stood. "Thanks."

Having a final glance around to make sure he had everything he came with, minus two children, Asher held Janie's hand and walked toward the door. He didn't check to see if Sean was following, but he heard a soft tread behind him, so assumed he was.

SEAN

Sean followed Asher and Janie out to the car, a little dumbstruck by how clever that little girl was. He didn't know much about kids—he hadn't thought they were able to read at such a young age, but there she was reading a book like it was second nature.

Sean couldn't believe how his day had gone so far. This morning had been standard, one quick visit and some paperwork at the office. Then he turned up for his appointment with Asher at one o'clock and the rest —well, just unexpectedly strange and strangely wonderful at the same time.

He watched Asher as he opened the car doors and settled Janie into the seat, strapping her in safely. Sean walked around to the other side, assuming Asher himself would drive back and sank into the passenger seat, resting his head against the back.

Sean admitted to himself the visit to the hospital hadn't been as bad as he'd expected, but it was probably due to being distracted by Asher and the kids. *Poor Enrico must have a huge headache by now*, he thought.

He rolled his head on the headrest when Asher opened the driver door and settled in behind the wheel. Glancing at him, Asher said, "Are you okay? That was an awful big sigh there." His mouth kicked up at the corner.

Sean smiled at him. "Yeah, I'm okay. I think I'm just crashing slightly from the stress of being in there." He indicated to the hospital. "I'm fine though. How are you doing?"

Asher blew out a breath, facing forward and resting his hands on the wheel. "I'm worn out to be honest. I never feel much stress, except when one of the kids I look after is poorly or hurt." He shook his head. "I can't explain it. It's a different type of worry to what you feel looking after your own." He turned back to Sean and smiled. "Never mind. Let's get you back to your car. Bet you can't wait to get away from us and the drama."

"Nah, it's been okay." Sean fastened his seat belt as Asher started the car.

"Yeah, sure. You come for an appointment to discuss a conversion and end up in the last place you want to be at for over an hour!" Asher laughed, starting the short journey.

"We had a conversation about it. We managed to make some headway on what you want. I can't ask for more really."

"Well, I suppose there is that."

They were silent for a little while, during which time Sean watched the scenery. It wasn't very often he was a passenger in a car, only because he preferred to drive. Some people thought he might be scared to be in a car after his parents' accident, but he wasn't. Now alcohol, he abstained from religiously. No one would ever get hurt from his lack of inhibitions, not when he could prevent it.

He hadn't even noticed when they had pulled on to Asher's driveway, it was only when the engine stopped that he took note of where they were.

"Sorry, kinda spaced out there," he said with a laugh.

"It's okay. It gave me time to recharge a little, ready for the mini tornado that will happen when I let her free." Asher thumbed towards the back seat and grinned, making his face look much younger. Not that he was old to begin with.

Sean laughed as he got out of the car. "I'm sure that description is apt!" As he walked around the front of the car towards Asher, he scanned the garage. He could see it had so much potential, he just needed to get a peek inside before he could make any judgement.

He stopped at the corner, examining the front then the side of the garage, trying to determine approximate sizes when he felt a tugging on his trouser leg. He turned, gazing down and saw Janie stood next to him.

"Do you want to see my bedroom?" she asked, large blue eyes peering up at him.

"No, Janie, Sean doesn't want to see your bedroom. He has to go, sweetheart." Asher stopped next to them, smiling apologetically at Sean. "I'm sorry, she has no boundaries."

Resting a hand on Janie's small shoulder, Sean replied, "Maybe I could have a look another day." He didn't intend to go into her bedroom at all, but he knew it would put her off for a while—it worked just as well on children as it did on adults.

Asher walked towards the house, talking over his

shoulder to Sean. "Look, I just wanted to apologise for what happened today. I know you said earlier, it was okay, but it really wasn't. You wasted your time and probably missed appointments. I'm really sorry you got dragged into this." Asher rested his hand on Janie's hair as she leaned against him.

"Honestly, it's fine, don't worry about it. This is one of the more adventurous appointments I've had. Several clients had me drinking tea and chatting to make sure I was someone they liked. It helps some people to get to know me before deciding whether they can work with me." Sean shrugged, glancing over at the garage again.

"Do you have time to have a quick look around it?" Asher asked as he unlocked the front door and ushered Janie inside.

"No, you said you were worn out, I can call to rearrange with you." Sean did want to see inside, for his own curiosity more than anything, but it could wait.

"It's fine. If you have the time, we can have a look. Really." Asher indicated for Sean to follow him into the house.

Sean walked into the entryway, again amazed by the condition of the property. "Only if you're sure," Sean replied to Asher's remark.

"Yes, we're fine. Let me just get Janie situated with her favourite film and I'll show you through." Asher turned and locked the front door before heading for the lounge. Sean walked over to the wooden bannister, running his hand along, feeling the workmanship involved. Zak would be very impressed with this work.

Asher returned, smiling when he saw Sean at the woodwork. "It's nice, isn't it? I had it refinished just over a year ago, and I think it matches the flooring well." Asher blushed a little at his words, but Sean wholeheartedly agreed and told him so.

"Thanks. Well, let's go see the garage." Asher walked purposefully towards the kitchen and unlocked the back door, before heading through. Sean followed, amazed again by how well the house had been looked after, even though he had briefly seen it before. He would have said he never made judgements before seeing something, but even he realised he never expected this from the outside. Asher knew his stuff.

Asher headed for the side garage door, unlocked this as well and indicated for Sean to enter. "It's just a storage place at the moment, so all of this stuff will be gone."

Sean inspected around, seeing boxes—some open, some taped shut—gardening equipment, outdoor toys and a whole host of other items. He walked around the places he could get to, investigating the inside space, bricks and the other side of the main garage doors.

He nodded to himself and murmured, "Yes, this could work."

"Do you think it's possible? What I want?" Asher's

questions broke into the silence.

"Yeah, definitely. I see a lot of potential in the space here. I'll obviously have to take measurements and thoroughly check out specific parts, but I don't see why it won't be possible."

"Brilliant." Asher smiled wide, and Sean lost his thoughts for a minute. Asher's straight white teeth were surrounded by full red lips and black stubble. He was stunning.

He shook his head. "Um, I'll come up with rough sketches for you and some approximate costings and get them across to you if that's okay?"

"Yes, sure. That's great. Thank you." Asher tripped over his words.

"Okay, well I'll leave you to your evening and get out of your hair." Sean walked towards the exit, past Asher. He had realised he needed to get away—Asher's smile was deadly, and he didn't like it. He didn't like it at all.

If his abrupt departure confused Asher, he didn't show it. Sean said goodbye at the front door and said he'd be in touch soon, then turned and almost ran for his car. He headed straight home, not bothering to head to the office. He knew he wouldn't be able to concentrate anymore.

It was only when he got home that he realised he had left the folder of information on Asher's kitchen counter.

CHAPTER FOUR

ASHER

Asher had hardly slept the previous night. Intermingled with his worry over Enrico were dreams about Sean and him in compromising positions. Neither made for a restful night.

He sat at the kitchen table nursing his third coffee, listening to the conversations between three of the older children before they went on the school run. It was eight-fifteen and shortly they would have to make the quick trek to the primary school.

Asher had to drop off seven children of varying ages, before heading home to wait for little Leo to arrive. Janie was already playing with Cooper. Today, they were heading for a long, hopefully tiring, walk then they would come back for lunch and naps.

Finishing his coffee, Asher stood and rinsed his mug in the sink. "Hey, guys, can you round up the rest of the kids for me, please. We need to get ready to leave," he asked.

"Sure, Asher." The children stood, collecting their belongings and traipsing into the lounge. He heard them telling the others to get their things.

The walk to school was the same as always, quick and simple. Asher really did have a good bunch of kids, which he would be eternally grateful for.

Walking back through the front door, Asher heard his mobile ring, and he grabbed it from his pocket. Seeing it was Martine, he answered as cheerfully as he could. "Hey, you! Good morning!"

"Morning, Ash. How are you?" Martine was chipper as always.

"Yeah, I'm all right. We're heading to Lammas today. You up for a walk? If the rain holds off, I might even let them splash in the water." Asher would like the company, and he also wanted to speak with Martine about what happened with Enrico.

"You sound strange. What's wrong?"

He could never get past that mother's intuition of hers.

"I'm fine, but there was an incident yesterday. I want to talk it over with you if you're free." He moved closer to the lounge to see what the kids were doing. Asher didn't want to say too much over the phone in case Janie and Cooper heard. He didn't want them worrying.

"Okay, sure. We'll be there. What time are you leaving?" Martine was happy to be out and about with the children, as was Asher. It was much better for them than sitting in the house all the time.

"As soon as Leo gets here." Asher squinted at his watch. "So, about ten minutes."

"Okay, see you there." Martine rung off without a goodbye—her natural exit; she didn't like goodbyes. Asher shook his head, chuckling whilst he strode to the lounge to check through his bag.

Fifteen minutes later, he was ushering the three children to the car, buckling them in and heading off. It was a large area of woods and open spaces alongside the River Cam. It also hosted a playground and an outdoor swimming pool.

The journey took less than ten minutes, and as he waited in the car park for Martine, he thought about why he was so worried about the incident with Enrico. He knew he'd done exactly what he should have done, so he had nothing to be concerned about legally. But he couldn't help it.

Martine pulled up right next to him, and they both set about getting the children ready for their walk. Asher's kids were pretty easy: Janie could walk by herself, Cooper and Leo were both two and could walk short distances, but Asher had the pushchair for when they got tired as he knew they would.

As they began their walk, Martine started straight in. "Okay, so what happened?"

Asher explained everything that had happened, excluding the parts about Sean until Janie piped up, "You had Sean to help too, didn't you, Uncle Asher?"

He closed his eyes, wincing when he realised just how much Janie had revealed with that one sentence.

"Who is Sean, sweetheart?" Martine asked Janie in a sickly-sweet voice, which had Asher gritting his teeth and shaking his head.

"He came around to see Uncle Asher then he took us to the hospital. And when Enrico was better, he came home with us." With that information, Janie skipped off ahead.

Martine chuckled. "Really? Well, that's interesting. Care to share, Ash?" He glared over at her, seeing her smirking.

He rolled his eyes. "Remember I mentioned the architect? Well, that's Sean. He came for his appointment, and that was when Enrico had his fall. He offered to drive us to the hospital, which I was more than grateful for."

"Ooh, tell me more."

"There's nothing really to tell. We sat in the waiting room for Sarah to finish up with Enrico and the doctor, then I drove him back to my house to fetch his car."

"And….?"

"And nothing. What do you think happened! I

allowed him to have a look around the garage when we got back, and then he hightailed it out of there, saying he'd get some plans to me next week." Asher tried not to sound petulant about that. He still didn't understand why Sean had disappeared as fast as he had.

"Firstly, you have nothing to worry about with Enrico. You followed all the policies correctly; you did what needed to be done. You have to forgive yourself. You can't beat yourself up every time something happens to someone. It was not your fault."

"But I was supposed to be watching him—"

"And you did. Every parent and childminder and uncle and aunt and any other adult looking after children will, at some point, have to answer the door or answer the phone or just generally be away from the children for a few seconds. You did nothing wrong." Martine put heavy force behind her words, and Asher could feel them finally penetrate his fear.

He nodded to her. "Thanks."

"Secondly, Sean? Nice. See what he comes up with for the garage, and then see what happens." Martine waggled her eyebrows. "He might not even be gay!" She laughed.

"I am not chasing after Sean. He's the architect, and that's it, nothing more." Asher stared resolutely ahead.

"If you say so."

Asher caught her smirk out the corner of his eye and shook his head with a slight smile.

SEAN

Sean fell back onto the bed, bouncing slightly as Asher crawled closer. His eyes fluttered when Asher claimed his lips with a hard, hungry kiss, resting on his elbows to stop his backward momentum. Asher's hands cupped his face as the kiss deepened, invading his mouth with his tongue.

Gasping for breath, they pulled apart. Without pausing, Asher stripped off Sean's shirt and began kissing down his neck, biting gently where it met his shoulder. Soothing the sting with little laps of tongue, Asher continued the journey, licking at his pecs until reaching his nipples.

Sean was very sensitive and flinched, lying back completely when Asher flicked his tongue over his nipples repeatedly. "Fuck, Ash!" Asher moved to the other nipple, sucking and biting, making it so hard it hurt before taking his exploration further.

"God! Mmm." Undulating with pleasure as Asher tongued down his abdomen, Sean had the forethought to grab the hem of Asher's shirt, allowing him to pull it up the further down Asher went until it was finally off.

He threw it on the floor and ran his hands through Asher's hair.

He felt Asher's fingers at the button of his jeans, and he lifted his hips in approval, almost shouting, "Yes!"

Sean peered at Asher when he chuckled and saw his pupils were blown with pleasure despite his laughter. Asher made slow work of opening his jeans, flicking the button open and kissing the skin that was shown. Then he dragged the zipper slowly down, the sound loud in the quiet room. "Asher! Just do it!" Sean ran out of patience, batted Asher's hands away and unzipped quickly, opening the gap as wide as it would go.

Sean almost jumped off the bed from the heat of Asher's mouth as it descended onto his covered cock. "God!" Asher held the head in his mouth, tonguing the material wet and blowing out hot air, making Sean go cross eyed. "Fuck!"

Sean rested his head back and closed his eyes as Asher lifted off him. Opening his eyes again, he saw Asher move off the bed before grabbing Sean's jeans and briefs and pulling them off, yanking Sean to the edge of the bed at the same time.

"Mmm, just where I like you," Asher mumbled as he stared at Sean, eyes roaming across his naked body. Sean sat up, reaching for Asher's trousers not wanting to waste any more time. He quickly disposed of the clothes until Asher was as naked as he was. "In a hurry?" laughed Asher.

"Shut up," he replied without heat, at least not the angry kind. Sean lifted a hand towards Asher's cock, but Asher stopped him with a hand on his wrist.

"No. Your turn," he said, pushing Sean backwards on the bed again. Asher followed him until Sean was spread on the bed, and Asher was kneeling between his legs. "God, you look fucking amazing spread out for me like that."

Sean blushed, and Asher trailed a finger along the rosy patches no doubt lighting his cheeks and chest. Sean's eyes closed again as Asher's finger strayed to his nipples once more. "Fuck!" he breathed.

"You're so sensitive there. It's beautiful to watch," Asher said with gravel in his voice. "Absolutely beautiful."

Sean felt Asher trail fingertips down his abdomen, following to the base of his cock before wrapping around and squeezing gently.

"Oh fuck! Asher!" He bucked into Asher's hand with that gentle touch.

Gripping Sean's cock had him lifting again, and Asher began to stroke up and down, playing close attention to just under the head of his cock. Sean watched as Asher repositioned himself on his stomach before leering at Sean with heat in his eyes.

"Mine!" Asher said before he engulfed the whole of his cock in his mouth.

"Shit!" Watching Asher as he sucked Sean's cock made the pleasure ramp higher. Asher flicked at the underside, the strip of highly sensitive nerves just beneath the hood of his cock, and Sean almost flew off the bed. "Oh, my fucking god!"

He calmed a little as Asher withdrew from the area, then tensed again as Asher began swallowing his cock, sucking and tonguing the slit each time. Sean wasn't going to last long at this rate.

"Ah, Ash, that's…Oh, god! Just like that!" Sean couldn't help but grab a handful of Asher's hair. He tried to keep still, but he couldn't help moving his hips in time with Asher's strokes until Asher rested his forearm across his abdomen to stop him. Flinging his head back against the bed, he groaned as Asher's strokes increased in speed.

"Ash. I'm gonna come! Fuck! Asher!" Sean felt Asher flick his tongue repeatedly over the tip and underside of the head of his cock, and he was done. "Fu-uck!"

Sean woke as his abs contracted with his orgasm, and his release spilled over his hand and stomach. "Oh, fuck!" He groaned out the last of his orgasm, then relaxed into his bed, sprinkled with sweat. "Shit!" He laid there breathing heavily in the dark silence of the night, wishing his mind had not taken him on a ride with his—admittedly gorgeous—client. "Shit!" he repeated, shaking his head.

He swung his legs over the edge of the bed and rested his head in his clean hand. His mind was a mess; he had so many thoughts going round his head, he didn't know which way was up. He needed a shower, though.

After towelling off, he finally thought to check the clock: two o'clock. Saturday morning. There was no way he was going back to sleep after that. Sean got dressed in joggers and a t-shirt and went to his study. He could get some work done as he was up.

Eight hours later, Sean uncoiled from his desk, stretching his arms towards the ceiling, and heard his back crack and creak from the time spent curled over the paperwork. His stomach rumbled, and he realised he hadn't stopped for breakfast like he'd planned to. It happened more often than it should; as soon as ideas started to hit his brain, everything else went by the wayside.

He'd made good progress on a couple of aspects of the project. He needed to prepare a couple more variations before he would be ready to show Asher what he had. If he could even face him after *that* dream. Sean blushed just thinking about it, and there was no one there to see him.

Standing abruptly, he stalked towards the kitchen to make some coffee and toast. Adding a bowl of mixed fruit, some yogurt and the necessary cutlery to a tray, Sean waited for breakfast to be ready before taking it back to his desk. He should really eat it at the table, but he was eager to continue his work.

He ate his way through his toast as he poured over the notes he had already written, making sure to double check the figures. It was only an estimate at this point because he hadn't had the chance to take measurements, but he was good with guessing and didn't think he'd be far off.

Throughout the rest of the day, Sean remembered to eat the fruit and yogurt and finished the flask of coffee he had brought in with him. He stopped for dinner when his stomach protested again, then went right back to his work.

Sean's body was tight with tension by the time he had decided enough was enough for that day. He checked the clock and was shocked to see it was ten at night. He'd worked on this for twenty hours. Shaking his head, he stood up with difficulty and walked through to his kitchen. He grabbed a couple of bottles of water, drank one and rested the other on his bedside table. Lying back, he stared at the ceiling.

Next thing Sean knew, light was blazing through

his curtains. Groggily, he rubbed his eyes and face, trying to see well enough to focus on his clock. It took him a few tries, but eventually he realised it was eleven. He hadn't slept that long in a while.

He groaned, wanting to go back to sleep but knowing he had to do his gym workout. He'd missed it yesterday, but he wasn't going to do that today. Hauling himself out of bed, he got himself ready and hit his renovated gym—a converted bedroom which had all the gym equipment he used. He could have gone out to a gym, but he liked being able to use whatever equipment he wanted, whenever he wanted, instead of having to wait for someone to finish with it.

Ninety gruelling minutes later, Sean felt refreshed even before his shower. He'd needed to work out the kinks in his joints and muscles from being in the same position most of the previous day. Having showered, refuelled and stocked up on snacks, Sean headed once again for his study.

In the zone, it took a while for Sean to realise someone was pounding on his front door. He blinked as he glanced up from his work. What was all that about?

Heading to the door, he opened it rather fast, and Max strode in.

"Finally! I thought you'd probably died in here and nobody would have found you for weeks!" Max was a whirlwind—he took no prisoners.

"As you can see, I'm still alive. What's up?" Sean was used to Max turning up unannounced but not bulldozing in like he had this time.

Max was gorgeous, there was no other word for it. He was the epitome of tall, dark and handsome. Short black hair, slightly longer on top with a thin beard and moustache surrounding his full lips. Max looked after himself, religiously attending a gym, or Sean's gym, every day and running and swimming as often as he could.

At one point in their past, Sean thought he'd had the hots for Max. He soon realised they were not compatible and threw the thought aside, concentrating on their friendship. Not that he'd had any choice in the friendship department.

It was Max that had eventually persuaded Sean to use his parents' insurance money to pay for his university fees. Max had used the parent card: "What if they are peeking down on you right now? Would they want you to be worried about making ends meet? Or would they want you to have a fulfilling life doing something you love without having to worry about the cost? I never met them, but I bet I know what they'd say."

With that, it was a done deal.

"I've been trying to get a hold of you all day! What have you been doing?"

"Shit! I've not checked my phone for the last two days. I don't even know what time it is!" Sean walked to his bedroom to collect his phone from the bedside table. Unplugging it, he saw thirty-six text messages and seventeen missed calls, all from Max.

"It's eight!" Max shouted from the direction of the kitchen. No doubt he was hunting for food.

"I didn't realise how long I'd been working." Sean couldn't believe how quickly the time had gone. "I've been working on a new project, and I got sucked in." Sean shrugged.

"Yeah, yeah. I know the drill. What're you working on?" Max raided the fridge as he talked, pulling out some meat and salad and grabbing the bread.

Watching Max make a sandwich with his food, Sean carried on talking. "It's a two-car garage conversion into a childminding space. I need to speak to you about it because it needs some fine tuning to be what Ash—the client wants it to be." Sean thought he caught his slip in time, but typically, Max heard it.

"Ash? Ash, who?" Max stared at Sean and smirked.

"The client is called Asher," Sean reluctantly shared.

"Ooh, first name terms already. When did you see him?" Max finished creating his sandwich masterpiece and took a big bite. "Actually, wait with that info. Go and get dressed, we're heading to Crush."

"I'm not in the mood, Max."

"Yes, you're going. No arguments. Now, get gone."

Max smiled and looked like a hamster with his cheeks full of food.

Sean knew it was no good. He shook his head, rolled his eyes and went to get changed.

Twenty minutes later, they were off. Max didn't mention anything about Asher during the ride, but Sean knew better than to think the subject had been dropped. And he was right. When they had been seated with drinks—a soft drink for Sean—Max carried on as if the gap between parts of the conversation had never happened.

"So, when did you see this Asher?" Max asked as he took a swig of his beer.

"Thursday. I went to his house for the initial meeting, but it kinda went crazy and didn't go to plan." Sean felt the story spill out of him as it always did when Max was asking questions. "One of the children he was looking after fell off a chair in the kitchen while he was answering the door. I drove them all to the hospital and stayed to help him. Then when we got back to his house, I had a quick look round the garage to get some ideas. That's what I've been working on all weekend."

It was an abridged version of the events, but it got the point across.

Sean glanced over when Max hadn't said anything and found Max staring at him as if he'd grown another head. "What?"

"You willingly went to a hospital? You stayed at said hospital for an undisclosed amount of time?" Max's eyebrows were in his hairline, eyes wide with disbelief. "Who are you and what have you done with Sean?"

"Ha ha, very funny." Sean was not amused.

"I'm sorry, but—" Max blew out a breath. "That's big, Sean. Massive! You've not been in a hospital since your parents died. You always avoid glancing at it when we drive past it. And here you are telling me you not only went into it, but you stayed there for a while." Max shook his head.

"I know, I know. It's just—" Sean paused. "I was freaked out when I first walked in there, but I had this kid in my arms—"

"Wait, what? What kid?" Max interrupted.

"The boy who fell off the chair. Asher had three kids with him at the time, and he was trying to hold the boy and keep hold of the hands of the two girls. I offered to carry the boy."

Max blinked and shook his head again. "Okay, carry on."

"So, I was carrying the boy and didn't want to worry him so although I was freaked, I was also…not. I don't know how to explain it." Sean struggled to find the words to describe how he felt. "When we sat in the waiting room, I could feel myself getting worked up, but Asher seemed to distract me with talk. We had a conversation about the conversion, and before I knew it, we were heading back to Asher's house."

"Wow. Amazing that it was a guy that got you to go into a hospital!" Max joked, and he knew Max was trying to lighten the mood.

"Shut up, moron!" He shook his head. The rest of the evening passed by in a blur of conversation and drinks.

CHAPTER FIVE

ASHER

The weekend had been a nice break for Asher. They had spent Saturday at the zoo. Though he had done it with the childminded kids before, it was simpler with just one child, especially as Janie was easier to care for than most four-year olds. On Sunday, they just relaxed around the house and garden.

Sarah had given him a call and told him Enrico was fine. She said he was being his usual self, and there hadn't been any complications. Asher, even though he had spoken with Martine and had reduced his worry a lot, felt the final weight leave his shoulders.

He'd had a conversation with Janie about why she had been so upset when Enrico had hurt himself. She said she didn't like seeing him upset when she couldn't help. Asher decided Janie must be sensitive to other people's emotions and reassured her that it was fine to feel however she needed to.

Monday crept up on him, and Asher had not wanted to get out of bed. His thoughts and dreams were still scattered with Sean's face, and Asher needed a rest from it. He hadn't heard anything from Sean since he'd left Thursday evening. Asher shook his head. He swung his legs to the side of the bed and stood.

Stretching his arms up, he yawned as he walked towards the bathroom for a shower. Turning the water on, he rolled his neck, waiting for it to warm up. He didn't mind cold showers but there was a time and place for one.

Stepping in, he groaned as the water hit his skin. He began to wash his hair then his body. He tried to ignore his morning wood, but it didn't seem to want to go away so he knew he needed to deal with it.

Rolling his eyes, he gripped his cock and started slow, hard strokes, gasping into the water when pleasure streamed through him. He wasn't responsible for where his mind drifted after that. He saw Sean on his knees in front of him, holding onto Asher's ass while his mouth worked Asher's cock.

"Fuck!" Asher whispered into the shower tiles, his closed eyes seeing Sean licking his cock then taking him deep again and again, using his hand to keep up the friction.

Desire coursed through his body faster than he

expected. Rotating his hand around the hood of his cock and stimulating the underside made his orgasm rush forward.

"Uncle Asher?" With those words, his climax became non-existent.

Asher's eyes flew towards the door, his breath rushing out of him, hoping Janie wouldn't enter. She knew not to when he was showering, but they had the rule that she could come in once the shower had turned off.

"Ye—" Asher's voice came out as a croak, so he cleared his throat and tried again. "Yes, Janie?"

"Can I have a croissant, please?"

"Yes, sweetheart. Go get one. I'll be out in a minute."

"Thanks!" He heard her footsteps retreat, then return. "Uncle Asher!"

"Yes?" Asher couldn't help but smile.

"Am I allowed to put the TV on, too?"

"Of course. Make sure you get a piece of fruit as well, please." Asher tried to keep her eating healthy, but it didn't always work, so he was happy to compromise. He remembered his mother having to do the same with Annie when they were younger. Like mother, like daughter.

He quickly washed his body, wincing at the sensitivity of his still hard cock, before stopping the shower and drying himself off. It was a good job Janie had interrupted. That shower was headed in the wrong direction for Asher's liking. He barely knew Sean, though he might feel differently once he got to know him, but not yet. He might not even be gay.

Muttering to himself, he got dressed and headed for the kitchen, hearing Janie in the lounge. Switching the coffee machine on and watching every drip of the coffee as it hit his mug made Asher realise it was going to be a long day.

Fifteen hours later, after a very long day of whingy children, putting a sleepy girl to bed and getting the house ready for the next day, Asher sat down and rested his head against the back of the sofa. He stared at the ceiling for a few minutes before getting the energy to reach for the remote. Just as he was about to turn the TV on, he heard a clatter outside. Frowning, he stood and walked to the covered windows. Even though there was still some light outside, he enjoyed the solitude of having the curtains closed once Janie was in bed; it made him feel like he was separated from the rest of the world.

Using one finger, he cracked the curtain a little so he could see into his front garden. He saw a figure walking near his garage. It crouched down to the ground, reached forward and stood up again. Asher saw the figure walk towards the front of the garage, and his car, and do the same thing there.

Puzzled, Asher went to his front door and threw it

open quickly enough to hopefully scare away whoever it was. "Oi! Get off my driveway!" he shouted at the figure, who promptly fell on their backside and dropped whatever they had in their hands.

"Shit, Asher! You scared the hell out of me!"

It took a minute to recognise the voice. "What the hell are you doing skulking around at this time of night?" Asher blew out a breath and tried to calm his heart rate.

Sean gathered his papers—that was what he had dropped when he had fallen—and walked over to Asher. "I'm sorry, I was trying to get some measurements so I could finish creating some designs, but I've been busy all day, this was the only time I could get here. I thought you'd probably be in bed, so I thought I'd just do the outside ones for now and come back tomorrow for the inside ones." Sean's words came tumbling out in rapid sequence.

Asher paused, making sure Sean had finished what he was saying. "And you thought creeping around at ten at night made sense?" He raised his eyebrows at Sean. Sean had dark circles below his eyes and deeper lines than before in his forehead. Asher wondered if something was stopping him from resting. Shaking his head, he indicated inside. "Never mind. Come on in, I'll make us some coffee."

He turned and walked towards the kitchen, assuming Sean would follow him. As he made some fresh coffee, he pulled out the plate of cheesecake Martine had brought around earlier that day and placed it on the table. He pulled out two plates, two forks and a knife. Cutting two slices, Asher placed them on separate plates and returned the cheesecake to the fridge.

Sean had yet to say a word, so Asher continued making the coffee and, when it was ready, placed the drinks and cheesecake in front of Sean, then sat opposite him.

Looking him straight in the eye, he said, "So, why can't you sleep?"

Sean flinched as if Asher had hit him, and he felt bad for being so abrupt.

"Sorry, it's none of my business." Asher glanced down at his plate and picked up his fork. He doubted he would taste a thing, but it was a distraction.

"It's okay. I—" Sean paused, and Asher glanced up. "I get like this sometimes when I have a project that inspires me; Max says it consumes me. I can't think properly until the work is done to my satisfaction. It's both a curse and a blessing." Sean took a drink, and Asher watched his throat muscles work as he swallowed.

Feeling his cock fill at the sight, he cleared his throat to remove any potential sound of arousal. Asher responded, "Who is Max?" He wasn't sure if he hoped Sean would say his boyfriend because then it meant he was gay, or that Max was a colleague because Asher didn't want Sean to be attached. His mind was all over the place, mainly in his cock.

"Max is a friend. He's an interior designer I met while I was at uni. We work together on a lot of projects really. I've helped his business, he's helped mine." Sean smiled, appearing younger and less tired with it.

"I don't know much about architecture. How long were you at uni?"

"Seven years in total, but three of those were work experience with TAC."

"Wow, you must definitely enjoy it to go through that amount of time. You said you met Max there?"

"Not actually at uni but while I was there. He was at a different uni, and we met randomly at a bar one Christmas. He hasn't left me alone since!" Sean said this with a laugh.

"He sounds like a good friend." Asher was glad there was someone in Sean's life that could help him when he needed it.

"He is, even when I don't want him to be." Sean laughed.

"Is there just Max in your life or do you have other friends and family?" Asher closed his eyes and cursed inwardly as the question came out, remembering their conversation from the hospital. "Shit, sorry, you did tell me about your parents. I'm really sorry. Me and my big mouth." He shook his head for being such an insensitive asshole.

"It's okay." Sean took a drink of his coffee. "I don't have any other family, but I do have a couple of close friends. Zak had a baby last year, so I don't see much of him at the moment. He's a woodworker—he would love the work done in your hallway," Sean said, indicating behind him. "He'd be really impressed with the work."

"Zak King?" he asked.

"Yeah!" Sean seemed surprised.

Asher smiled. "Zak is the one who did the work. Small world."

"Wow, yeah it is." Sean glanced down at his cheesecake then back up at Asher. "He'd definitely love the work then. He's always been a fan of his own stuff." Sean chuckled, then took a bite of the cheesecake. "Oh my god!"

Asher laughed. "You like the cheesecake then?" He tried to adjust himself discreetly; the noises Sean made did nothing to ease his hard-on.

"Goh, oo maye iss?" Asher burst out laughing as Sean tried to talk with his mouth full. Sean flicked his eyes towards Asher, and he saw the blush redden Sean's cheeks. He stopped laughing as he watched the flush darken and move down Sean's neck. He hardened completely in his jeans as his breath began to come more rapidly. Asher was overwhelmingly aroused by the sight of Sean looking flushed with a mouth full of cake. Inappropriate images flashed through his mind.

Asher swallowed, trying to get some moisture to talk. He blinked his eyes away, afraid to watch for any longer and stood abruptly, turning to the coffee machine again. "More coffee?" His voice was hoarse, and he cleared his throat several times as he went about making more coffee even though Sean hadn't answered. He was afraid to turn around, scared at what he might find, although he wasn't sure why. He didn't know if he wanted Sean to be getting ready to leave or staying where he was.

He wished he could understand what it was about Sean that had him twisted in knots. He had been attracted to other guys before—he was gay after all—but Sean threw him off base. Was it because they had both lost someone close to them? Asher wasn't sure, but he didn't think so.

Thinking back to their initial meeting, in the few seconds before Enrico's accident, Asher remembered feeling an instant attraction to Sean. He was gorgeous, and though he looked younger than Asher, he had an older feel to him. Probably due to everything he had been through.

Asher finished doctoring the coffee and, taking a deep breath, turned to the table, not afraid to face Sean now his erection had calmed.

He didn't peek at Sean until he placed the coffee on the table and sat down. Pushing Sean's towards him, he glanced up, almost knocking the mug over when he saw heat flickering in Sean's eyes. Then he noticed the frown Sean was wearing.

"You okay?" he asked, puzzled.

Sean blinked at him, before shaking his head but staying quiet.

"If you want to talk...?" Asher left the door open for Sean if he wanted to. He decided to go back to what they were saying before the cheesecake. "Yeah, um, Zak did the work before his baby was due. I remember him telling me it was nearly time, and that if —was it Ashley?—went in labour, he would have to finish it later." He took a sip of his coffee. "Luckily for both of us, he managed to finish before."

Sean's eyes seemed to have cleared while Asher had been talking. "Yeah. I remember hearing Ashley complain that if the baby didn't get here soon, she was never going to let Zak near her again. I don't know anything about having children, but I know she hated being so uncomfortable."

"Yeah, Annie was the same. She complained throughout the pregnancy that Janie was going to be huge, and when she went over her due date, she was almost inconsolable." Asher snorted. "She was over the moon when Janie arrived though." He smiled fondly at the memory of the first time he saw Janie in Annie's arms. It was a memory that was never caught on camera, but he would forever see in his head.

"I don't know how you do it." Sean's remark brought him out of his memories.

Asher scrutinised him. "What do you mean?"

Sean peered down at his empty plate as he answered. "How can you look at Janie every day and not see death and pain?" Sean's gaze found his again, and the pain in them was astounding.

Asher wasn't offended, in fact, his heart cracked open in sympathy. "I see the beauty of a child who is alive, who, although has no memory of her mother, will forever know who she was through pictures, videos and memories from me." He wanted to envelope Sean in his arms and get rid of his suffering. "I see the face of my sister in Janie every day, which reminds me that Annie is here with me, even when she isn't. I don't see anything but love and beauty when I look at that girl."

Sean studied him, tension bracketing his eyes. "I had to sell their house because I couldn't face the memories. They became overrun by feelings of hatred and anger." Sean stopped himself, eyes wide, as though he hadn't meant to say that, which he confirmed with his next words. "Sorry, I didn't mean to lay that on you." He shifted uncomfortably, and Asher was worried he was going to leave.

"It's okay to say what you want. There's no right or wrong way for you to feel."

"So I'm told." Sean paused. "Max helped me see I needed to live my life instead of just going through the motions. Doesn't always work. God, I'm so sorry. This has become way deeper than it should." Sean tried a half-hearted chuckle.

SEAN

Sean couldn't believe he had just laid all that on Asher, a stranger. He needed to leave, but Asher's quiet words stopped him from standing.

"Sometimes you meet someone who makes it easy to talk. Maybe you feel comfortable enough with me to do that." Asher gave a small smile. "I'm happy to listen. And help if I can."

Sean gazed at him for a moment, then smiled back. "Thanks."

He must have looked uncomfortable because Asher changed the subject. "Would you like to see the garage?" Asher got up and took their plates to the sink.

"That would be great, thanks." Sean picked up his things as Asher opened the back door. After Sean went through, Asher attached a small gate to the open doorway.

"Janie will know where I am if she wakes up," Asher explained without him asking.

They walked to the garage, and Asher flicked on the lights. Sean blinked at the brightness after being outside in the dark. He took another look around, walking the perimeter before taking out a pen and flicking open his folder. He made a mental note to get the rest of the paperwork from Asher later.

Sean made a few notes regarding the internal condition, the flooring and the roof, before taking out his digital tape measure. Standing at one end of the garage, he measured to the far side, and then did the same for the other direction, then floor to ceiling. Once he had the measurements, he noted them down.

"There, all done with the measurements. Tell me about where you envisage the different areas you want." Sean was in full work mode now, their previous discussion filed away, but not forgotten.

Asher wandered forward, gazing around. "Well, in my head, I see the shower and toilet to the rear of the garage. Then the kitchen along the far side. I was thinking it could maybe be U-shaped, so it appears separate." Asher was gesturing with his whole body as he described his vision, and Sean was mesmerised. "I see a door to the driveway on this wall here, where the parents can enter, and then a TV and sofa right near the front. The rest of it will all be open space for storage and tables and other stuff." Asher smiled when finished and gazed over at him. "What do you think?"

It took Sean a minute to respond—Asher was fascinating in his enthusiasm. "Sounds good." He cleared his throat and tried to say something that didn't sound stupid. "I'm not sure if we may have to move the kitchen over to the other side though; it depends on where the gas and electricity enters. Same with the shower and toilet, but I can investigate that." He wrote a note to remind him to check where the pipes were in the daylight. "Apart from that, the ideas are good. Would you like me to ask Max to come and look and quote you for the interior design? Or is that something you are planning to do yourself?"

"No, that would be great. I can do it myself, but I think it would disrupt my work too much. I was planning on getting someone else to outfit it, so yes, please."

Sean walked closer to Asher, intending to head back inside and go home. Asher didn't move as he approached, though their eyes stayed connected.

Stopping in front of Asher, he asked, "Is everything okay? Do you have any questions?"

Asher shook his head slowly and stepped closer. Sean had to lift his head slightly to keep eye contact. He searched Asher's eyes for something, though he didn't know what. He wanted Asher to kiss him, but he also didn't. He knew he didn't have the confidence to bridge the gap, and he was glad. He didn't know if he was ready for what might come from this.

He saw Asher lick his lips and raise his hand towards Sean's face, brushing a thumb down his jaw.

Sean's eyes fluttered at the touch, and he saw what appeared to be relief in Asher's eyes before his mouth descended onto his own.

The first brush of lips was tentative as if Asher was expecting to be pushed away, but when Sean didn't, Asher put his arms around his back and pulled him closer.

Sean had just enough time to move the papers to the side, so they didn't get squashed between them before Asher tilted his head and deepened the kiss. He moaned when Asher slid his tongue inside his mouth.

Sean was lost. It was like fireworks burst behind his eyelids. Asher tasted of cheesecake and coffee as addicting as the actual products. He dropped the papers on the floor as his arms automatically slid around Asher's waist, pulling him closer. He couldn't get enough of his taste.

Asher moved his hand to cup the back of his head when the kiss turned frantic. They kissed until they were both gasping for breath and had to pull back. Asher rested his head against Sean's as they breathed each other in.

Common sense began to invade Sean's mind. "I should—" Before he had chance to finish, Asher was kissing him again, turning him slightly and pressing him against the closest wall. Sean, yet again, lost his senses and began falling back under Asher's spell.

Breaking away to breathe, Sean moaned as Asher

kissed along his jaw to his ear, before nibbling on the skin beneath it, making him whimper and undulate against Asher.

Asher scraped his nails gently along Sean's side as he moved them towards his ass. Gripping firmly, Asher pulled him closer. Both groaned when their lower bodies touched, lighting more fireworks in Sean's nerve endings.

Sean pulled Asher's mouth back to his and kissed with more passion than ever.

They were kissing and dry humping each other like randy teenagers, but right then, Sean didn't care. He wanted more. He wanted whatever Asher would give him. He wanted everything. And that scared him. At that thought, he broke away and pushed at Asher's chest.

"I have to go." Asher released him from his embrace, and Sean slid out from the wall. Walking unsteadily over to the items he'd dropped, he picked them up and turned towards the door.

"Sean, wait!" Asher's voice was rough and ragged.

He didn't wait though. He walked out of the garage and towards the back door. Opening the gate—he'd seen how to do it when Asher had placed it there—he walked through the kitchen.

"Sean!" Asher called in a low voice. Sean assumed he didn't want to wake Janie up.

He stopped at the front door, hand on the knob.

Glancing back at Asher, he saw sadness in his eyes, but not regret, which eased Sean's heart a little. Though why he didn't know.

"Can I see you again? Not work related, I mean?" Asher seemed eager.

"That's not a good idea. I have to go." Sean turned the knob and opened the door, waiting again when Asher called his name.

"Wait, just a minute, please, just wait." Sean glanced back towards Asher to see him disappear into the kitchen, then return a few seconds later with the folder he had left the first day he was here. "You left these. I thought you might need them." Asher held them out, and Sean grabbed them. Asher wouldn't relinquish them to begin with, and Sean gazed at him. "Please, can I see you again?"

Sean's gaze roamed across Asher's face, committing the sight to memory. He already knew he wouldn't see Asher again. Tomorrow, he would be asking another architect to take over the project, but he wouldn't tell Asher that.

He shook his head. "No, sorry." He turned and walked out of the door.

Sean climbed into his car, breathing heavily, not from the walk but from the effort it had taken to not turn back. He threw the paperwork onto the passenger seat and drove off. His mind was in complete turmoil;

he didn't even remember the fifteen-minute journey home.

At least, he remembered to pick up the paperwork before heading inside.

Throwing himself onto the sofa, he stared up at the ceiling and placed his hands on his stomach. He blew out a breath.

"Shit." There was a lot of emotion exhaled with that one word: lust, pain, sadness, anger. But most of all: want. Sean had never felt as much as he had when he had been pinned against the wall by Asher. He felt *too* much.

And that was why he was going to ask someone else to take on Asher's conversion. He needed to stay as far away from him as possible. He would still ask Max if he wanted to do the interior, but he was staying well away.

Sean yawned, making his jaw crack. He needed sleep. He'd had very little since he'd met Asher and that had to change. He got ready for bed and was asleep the minute his head hit the pillow.

CHAPTER SIX

ASHER

He had stood in the hallway staring at the door for a long time after Sean had walked through it, hoping he would return. He couldn't understand why Sean had run. He hadn't meant to kiss him, but he'd been unable to resist. He couldn't deny the look of panic he had seen in Sean's eyes before he left though —that was the reason Asher had not gone after him.

He had debated calling the architecture firm and asking to speak with Sean because he didn't have his number yet but decided against it. He would wait until Sean next contacted him and see how it played out.

Asher heard his mobile ringing and pulled it from his pocket. The number was unknown. He didn't usually answer if he didn't know who it was, but something made him hesitate.

"Hello?" Asher answered.

"Good afternoon. Is that Mr Danvers?" said a pleasant, male voice.

"It is. Who's asking, please?"

"Sorry, it's Mike Calvert-Jones from Thompson Architect Company. I believe you have been dealing with Sean Edwards previously."

Asher frowned in confusion. "Yes, I have. Can I ask what this is about?"

"Of course! Sean has passed the project over to me to continue with. He said he had a few conflicting assignments and didn't believe he could give your project the amount of time it deserved."

Asher was silent for a moment. He couldn't believe what he'd just heard. Sean must be bailing out on the project because Asher kissed him.

"I'm sorry, Mr Thompson, there must be a mistake. No offence to you, but I don't want to work with anyone in your company except for Sean." He paused to let that sink in. "It's nothing against anyone else, but I've developed a good relationship with Sean and believe his vision for the conversion is excellent."

"Oh, has Sean given you his plans already? I didn't realise it was this far advanced." The architect was clearly flustered; Asher heard paper shuffling in the background.

"No, I've not received any drawn-up plans yet, but during our discussions, Sean's ideas were detailed, and I approve. I would like him to come back and continue if possible." Asher was laying it on a little thick, but he would not let Sean leave this project without a fight. He added another incentive. "I'm willing to wait until he has more time."

"I understand, Mr Danvers. Let me speak with Sean and see if we can come up with a solution that will make us all happy. Would it be okay for me to call you later today or tomorrow?"

"Yes, of course." He would much prefer if Sean called him.

"Thank you. Speak to you then, Mr Danvers. Bye."

"Thanks. Bye."

Asher turned the phone off and tried not to throw it across the room. He didn't really have any reason to be angry, but he was. He hadn't expected to feel a connection to Sean, to want to kiss him and protect him from pain. Asher was a little shocked himself at how much he wanted to keep Sean in his life. He had only known him for six days, after all.

He shook his head, watching the children play with the playdough. He hoped Mike Calvert-Jones was able to talk some sense into Sean, but he'd have to wait and see.

"Uncle Asher?"

Janie's voice pierced his thoughts, and he wandered over to her. "Yes, sweetheart?" He crouched down next to her chair, resting his arm on the back.

"Is Sean not helping with the building?"

Asher glanced at Janie. "Why do you ask that?"

"I heard you say you wanted him to come back."

Janie was as honest as every other child was at this age. Sometimes, though, they hit the nail on the head on a different scale.

"Yes, I did say that. I was saying that I would still like him to do the garage for us, but I'm not sure if he's going to have the time." He brushed her hair over her shoulder, away from the dough—he had experienced trying to wash it out of her hair before, and it was not pretty.

"I like him. He said I was clever for reading to him." Janie gazed at Asher and smiled. He saw Annie every time she did it. "He will come back, Uncle Asher. I know it."

He smiled back, leaning forward to kiss her cheek. "I like him too, sweetheart. How about we go out for lunch?" He stood and walked around the table to get ready to take three toddlers to a cafe.

He'd have to wait until he got the phone call before his mind would settle. And his heart.

SEAN

Sean had spoken to a colleague earlier that morning asking if he had space to take over Asher's project.

Mike had agreed with little explanation needed—he was always happy to take on more work. Sean had twisted the truth a little, saying he had too much on to do the project justice. It was a blatant lie, but Mike didn't know that.

He felt conflicted about the situation. On one hand, he loved the ideas he'd come up with for the conversion, but on the other hand, he needed to keep himself away from Asher.

He really didn't understand what it was about Asher that made him react so out of character. Usually, when he needed to take the edge off, he'd head over to a bar somewhere and pick up a random guy, but admittedly not very often. Then he'd be out of the door once their breathing had returned to normal.

He shook his head. He needed to get on with the work he did have, but he couldn't get Asher's plans out of his head. Checking his watch, Sean shook his head again, stood and picked up his wallet, phone and keys. Dialling Max as he was leaving, Sean got straight to the point.

"Distraction needed. Meet me at Pop's."

"Duly noted. See you there." Max was always more than happy to join him, but as Sean didn't usually call for this reason, he would know that something was wrong. Sean wasn't exactly sure what he would say to Max—he certainly wouldn't say the truth; he'd never hear the end of it.

Entering Pop's, Sean was met by a jingling bell and headed straight for the back—with it being only eleven o'clock, it was quiet, so he had plenty of tables to choose from—and picked his favourite spot. He was perusing the menu when he heard the bell jingle again. Glancing up, he saw Max enter, waving at Pop's daughter, Maria, as he passed.

He watched as Max weaved between the circular tables spaced around the room, stopping to admire the contents in the glass cases on his way. Sean loved Pop's. It was light, airy and arranged well within the available space. Sean couldn't have done any better and neither could Max. Pop's had the allure of freshly made food, such as salads and sandwiches, cooked meals, cakes and pastries, fresh coffee and different types of drinks.

Max dropped down in front of Sean, staring straight at him, eyebrows raised. "So, what's up, buttercup?"

Sean snorted into his menu. "Really? That's the best you could come up with?"

Max smiled a full Cheshire grin—he was so full of bullshit. He turned his attention to Maria as she approached the table. "Hey, Maria, how's things?"

"Bonny, thanks, Max, how're ya?" Maria was a quiet, Scottish woman who had always been a fixture here, as much as Pop had. Sean didn't know how old she was, but he did know that she had never been seen with anyone—some gossip he'd overheard once.

"I'm all right, thanks. Sean here, though, he's in a bit of a drama, so I'm trying to figure out what's wrong with him." Max's smile was contagious, and Maria grinned mischievously at Sean.

"Really? What's the issue?" Maria rested her hip against their table, studying Sean as if he was about to spill his guts. Sean shook his head and peered at the menu, even though he'd already decided what he was having.

"Guy problems," Max disclosed. Sean gawked at him in surprise. *How the hell did he know that?* Max smirked at him. *Shit, he didn't, my reaction just told him.*

Sean slumped back in his chair, rubbing his fingers across his forehead in annoyance.

"Oooh, Sean, tell all." Maria sat herself down next to Max, leaning her elbows on the table.

"There is nothing to tell, Maria. Max is mistaken." Sean tried his hardest to sound truthful, but by the looks on their faces, they weren't buying it.

Maria stood up again. "Ah, well. Let me take ya order then." She gave Max a wink. "Maybe it'll loosen ya tongue."

Max laughed. "Good luck with that! Okay, I'll have the cheeseburger and chips, please."

"Can you make that two, please, Maria. Thanks." Sean put the menu back in the holder and rested his hands in his lap. As Maria left, he peered at Max, seeing he was smirking at him again. "What?"

"You are so in over your head, and you don't even realise it." Max's expression turned serious. "You really like this Asher guy, don't you?"

"No, Max, I don't. And I've handed his project to Mike. He'll be able to do a good job with it." Sean stared down at his hands as his stomach rolled at the thought of not being able to see what happened with the conversion. Mike should have contacted Asher already to arrange another consultation.

Max raised his eyebrows. "I'm sure he will. But that just proves my point, doesn't it?"

"It doesn't prove anything."

"You've handed over a project, which, you admitted to me just a couple of days ago, you had spent probably thirty hours on. That's not a project you would usually just handover for someone else to finish. It proves to me that you are in over your head." Max leaned back against his chair as Maria brought their drinks. They hadn't ordered any, but having been customers on a regular basis, Maria knew their usual order.

"Here ya go, boys. Lunch will be out shortly." Although she gazed over at Sean sympathetically, she turned and went back to work. He had expected more questions, but the café was getting busier now it neared lunchtime.

"So, are you going to talk to me about it?" Max continued after taking a drink.

Sean debated what to say. He was staying away from Asher, so he didn't need advice. He didn't need the temptation of him. Nobody ever stays, so why should he be with someone who would eventually leave. Wasn't it better to just not be in the relationship to begin with?

"There's nothing to talk about. How's work?" Sean tried to change the subject.

Max sighed, shaking his head at Sean, but allowed the change. "It's good. I'm getting quite busy with the recommendations from TAC and from word of mouth. It's great." Sean was happy for him. Max had worked hard to get where he was, and although Sean had offered to pay for his university fees as well as his own, Max had told him a flat-out no because he wanted to do it himself. Sean understood that feeling because he had been the same.

"I knew it would take off. I'm glad I could help." He was careful not to remind Max about the new business from Asher. "How many are you doing—"

"Seriously, Sean? You couldn't talk to me yourself? You had to get someone else to call me to explain?"

Sean was interrupted by a line of questioning from a guy standing by their table. It took him a minute to register who it was.

"Asher?"

"Don't you Asher, me. What's going on?" Asher

stood there, holding a boy in his arms and two other kids by their hands.

He was about to answer when Janie jumped onto the seat next to him and threw her arms around his neck.

"Sean! I knew you'd come back! I told you, Uncle Asher! See, I told you!" Janie had a tight grip around Sean's neck, and he could feel himself sinking into her—she was a hard person to ignore, so he wrapped her in his arms gently.

"Hey, Janie." Sean watched Asher over Janie's shoulder and took in his angry face. Asher had definitely received a phone call from Mike, and he didn't look happy about it.

"Well?" Asher said with a little less anger.

"I'm busy with—" Sean started.

"Nope. Try again." Max snorted, reminding Sean he was there as a witness to this mess.

"You need someone—"

"Nope. Out of excuses yet?"

"Oooh, I like him." Sean could easily have smacked Max about the head for that comment. Pulling back from Janie, who hadn't seemed like she wanted to let go, Sean glanced up at Asher.

"You know why." He kept his gaze on Asher despite the blush that heated his cheeks.

Asher's gaze softened more. "Not really." He glanced across at Max, then back to Sean. "I know you were…" another glance to Max, "unhappy with the way we left things yesterday. I just want to understand why."

Janie left Sean's seat and walked over to Asher. "It's okay, Uncle Asher. Sean came back. He's not unhappy now." She hugged her arm around Asher's legs. "I'm happy he's back."

Sean swallowed hard at that. If he hadn't seen Asher in action prior to this, he would have believed Asher had put Janie up to this. But he knew this was just Janie being her very outspoken and honest self.

Max cleared his throat across the table, making a point.

"Sorry. Max, this is Asher Danvers. Asher, this is Max Hughes, the interior designer I mentioned before." The men nodded at each other.

"Nice to meet you, Max."

"You, too. I've heard a lot about you." Max smirked.

Asher raised his eyebrows, glancing at Sean in question. "Really? Good things, I hope?"

"Definitely." Max took on a professional tone. "I hear you're converting your garages to a separate unit. Sean has explained a little of what you are looking for, so if you'd like me to take a look, give me a call."

"Thanks, that'd be great." Asher glanced towards Sean again. "Well, we'll head to our table. But just so you know, I've told Mike no. I'm sure he'll be speaking with you later." With that bombshell, they moved away and took a table across the café by the window, which Sean could see had been prepared with a highchair and two booster seats.

Sean watched Asher get the children seated, seeing them smiling and laughing together. His heart pounded as he observed from afar, seeing a different scene with Asher and him in the same situation.

"You could have that, you know."

Max's voice splintered his vision, bringing him back to the present. He turned to look at him, seeing sympathy in his eyes.

"I don't know what you're talking about."

Maria chose that moment to bring over their food. "I waited until ya'd finished ya conversation. Didn't wanna interrupt."

"Thanks, Maria." Sean blew out a breath and began to eat his lunch. This had not turned out how he'd expected. So much for passing Asher's project off —looks like Mike will be seeking him out later.

Sean couldn't find it in himself to be upset about that.

CHAPTER SEVEN

ASHER

He had not heard anything from Sean since their meeting at Pop's, and that was three days ago. Although, he hadn't heard from Mike again, so he took that as a positive sign.

"Ash! Look!" Cooper shouted as he climbed up the steps to the small slide. He jumped at the top, making Asher's heart jump too.

"Sit down, Cooper! Remember you must go down the slide on your bottom!" Asher shouted back. He wasn't far away from him—he was pushing Leo on the swing just across from the slide. Unfortunately, Cooper was a bit of a daredevil, even at two years old, so Asher had to keep an eye on him.

Cooper sat down and giggled as he slid, bumping at the bottom. "Agay!"

"Yes, Cooper, you can go again." Asher's gaze went

to Janie who was sitting at the top of the bigger climbing frame, swinging her legs over the edge. She was cuddling with Albert bunny.

Asher's heart broke for her. They'd had a discussion this morning about Annie. It was her anniversary today, and Asher had sat Janie down and explained that they would look after the children as normal today, and then take some flowers and go and see Annie's grave later.

Janie still didn't really understand the significance of the grave. Last year, she had asked if her mummy was stuck under the ground, but Asher was quick to assure her that she wasn't. Asher had made the decision to explain in as simple terms as possible, so he'd told Janie that Annie was asleep in a bed under the ground, but she was free to fly in the sky whenever she wanted to. He'd also told Janie that Annie often watched what Janie was doing, both in the day and at night-time. And Janie could talk to her whenever she wanted to, and Annie would hear her.

He didn't want Janie scared for her mum or worried about death in general. So, he'd tried to explain it in a way she could understand.

She had been very quiet all morning, still playing with the other children, but a lot more subdued than usual, understandably.

His mobile rang and he picked it up, heart skipping

a beat when it came up as unknown again. Hoping it was Sean, he answered.

"Hi." Sean's hesitant voice flowed into Asher's ear, making him close his eyes in relief.

"Hey."

They paused for a moment, then both started talking at once.

"I'm sorry—"

"I didn't think—"

They laughed.

"You first," Asher said.

"Okay. I just wanted to say, I'm sorry. I know giving the project away was the coward's way. I just thought it would be the best option."

"You're back on it now?" Asher couldn't stop the hopeful note from entering his voice as he watched the children. Cooper and Leo had moved over to the sandpit, so he went and sat on the bench right next to it.

"Yes, I am." He blew out an audible breath. "Which is why I'm calling. We need to meet again to go over the plans I've created, and you need to decide which, if any, are what you want."

"Okay. Are you free now?"

"Now?"

"Yes, I'm at the park with the kids. We'll be here for a while yet. You're welcome to join us, and we can discuss it while they play."

Sean didn't say anything for a moment, and Asher thought he was going to refuse.

"Okay, where are you?"

Asher named the park, and Sean rang off saying he'd be there shortly.

Half an hour later, Sean walked up with a briefcase and a carrier bag. He sat down next to Asher, resting the carrier bag between them.

"Hi." Sean gazed at him; the apology written in his face. "I come bearing gifts." He indicated the bag.

Asher shook his head. "You didn't need to bring anything."

"Okay, well it's more gifts for the kids."

"Sean!" Janie came running up to Sean and jumped up on his knee, making him grab for her so she didn't fall. Janie threw her arms around his neck, just like she had done in the café.

"Hiya, Janie. You okay?"

"I'm sad."

"What's the matter?" Sean peered over at Asher because Janie was still clinging to him.

"We're going to see Mummy today." Janie moved and sat on Sean's knee, cuddling into his chest, holding Albert bunny tight.

Sean's eyes went wide, and Asher swore in his head. He should have prepared Sean for what today was—he honestly hadn't thought Janie would say anything, but he should have known better.

He mouthed, "Sorry," to Sean, who shook his head in return.

"Okay." Asher could see Sean was at a complete loss as to what to say.

"Hey, Janie. Sean brought a surprise." Janie's head popped up, making Asher laugh as she almost clocked Sean on the chin. "Would you like to see it?"

"Yeah!"

"Go and get Cooper and Leo, and we will all look."

Janie scrambled off Sean's legs and jumped into the sandpit, excitedly telling them to hurry up.

"I'm sorry, Sean, I should have told you what today was." Asher felt bad for throwing this at him unprepared.

"It's okay. I guess it's still difficult for me. I don't visit my parents except for on their anniversary." Sean gasped and glanced around wildly. "Sorry! I always seem to share too much when you're around." With that, Sean blushed bright red.

Inwardly, Asher smiled in triumph. "It's fine. Like I said before, you can talk to me about anything."

"No, you're a client. I can't get too involved."

"Says the guy who's brought gifts for the kids his client is looking after." Asher cocked his head, staring Sean straight in the eye.

Sean looked away when the kids appeared.

"What is it, Sean! What's the surprise?" Janie was so excited, she was bouncing on her toes.

Sean laughed, opening the bag. He brought out three child-sized water squirters in various colours, showing the children what they were and explaining how they worked.

"Uncle Asher! Can we have some water now?" Janie exclaimed.

Asher laughed, grateful for Sean's gift. "Not at the minute, sweetheart." He saw her face drop. "But as soon as we get home, we can take them out into the garden and fill them up. Is that okay?"

"Can we go now?"

He laughed again. "No, not right now. We've not been here too long. Let's play here a bit longer, then we'll go for lunch and water play this afternoon."

He saw she was about to protest again but glanced at him, and he saw when she realised she would not win the argument.

She huffed a breath. "Okay, Uncle Asher." She put the toy back in the bag. "For safe keeping."

Cooper and Leo were running around with their toys, waving them around in the air, before jumping into the sandpit with them. Janie walked over and joined them, seemingly happier for the moment.

"Thank you for that," Asher said.

"No problem. I wasn't sure if they'd be okay or get me into trouble with you, but it was worth the chance."

Asher peered over at Sean to see him smirking while watching the kids.

Shaking his head, he asked Sean about the plans.

"Yeah, hang on." He reached for his briefcase and removed a folder. "So, I have three different concepts for you to look at: the outside view and inside view. Have a look." He passed over the folder and Asher, while keeping one eye on the children, scanned over what Sean had created.

He was overwhelmed by what he saw. The designs were three-dimensional and almost jumped off the page. He could see exactly what Sean was getting at with each design.

"These are incredible."

"Thanks."

"I don't know if I can decide!" Asher liked something about every design he had done.

"Okay, well tell me what you like about what you see—or what you don't like. Both will help get a clearer idea of what you want in the end."

Asher studied the designs again. "I like where the windows and door are on this one. And the shower room on this one. I don't know if they can be combined?"

"Yeah, sure. That's why we go through this together, so we can see what you like and don't like, then combine them into something you love."

Asher glanced over at Sean, seeing him smiling at

Janie. Inspecting the sandpit, he saw Janie pulling faces at Cooper and Leo to get them to laugh.

"Would you like to come back to ours for lunch?" Asher wished he'd kept the question to himself when he saw Sean shut down.

"Sorry, I have to get back to work. I have two appointments this afternoon that I have to prepare for." Sean stood up, collecting his things. "Keep hold of the designs and let me know when you've had a chance to look through them properly."

Asher realised Sean was running again and tried to catch his arm before he went. "You don't need to run."

Sean paused, eyeing his bag. "Yeah, I do," he stated.

"Sean! Are you going?" Janie ran over, throwing her arms around Sean's legs.

"Yes, Janie. I have to go back to work."

"You will come back, won't you?" Asher saw Janie peek up at Sean and just knew she was giving him the puppy eyes. He hid his smile behind his hand.

"Um, yes, Janie. I'll come back." He awkwardly patted her back.

"Yay! Bye, Sean!" And off she ran, back to the sandpit.

"I'm glad, too," Asher breathed.

Sean peered at him but didn't say anything, pain reflected in his eyes once again. He turned and walked away. Taking another piece of Asher's heart with him.

SEAN

Why was walking away getting harder and harder to do? Sean's feet felt like lead as he walked back to his car. He hadn't lied to Asher, he did have two appointments this afternoon—only one of them was much later at Crush with Max, Zak and Ethan. He grimaced. He knew he would be getting the third degree about this situation with Asher because Max was sure to bring it up, making the others join in too.

His afternoon passed without incident—although not without thoughts of Asher—and soon he found himself on the way home. His thoughts constantly flitted back to Asher and Janie throughout the drive, and he found himself wanting to be with them during the roughest day of the year for them—or at least that's how he saw it. He hated that Asher had to deal with this alone and, although he would be of no use really, Sean wished he could help ease some of the burden.

He shook his head, reminding himself that he couldn't let his emotions cloud his judgement—he *knew* that Asher would leave him. Friends were easier, Sean never got close enough to let it bother him if they left him. He could take or leave them all. The rough cadence of his heartbeat belied his beliefs.

Parking on his drive, he glared up at the house that had been paid for with his parents' lives and wished they were here instead, even if it was a house he was proud of. *Maybe he could show Asher one day.* Thoughts turning towards his client made him jump out of the car and head towards the front door.

He threw his briefcase on the sofa as he passed, walking straight through to his shower room, shedding his clothes as he went—he'd pick them up later.

Yanking the temperature as hot as he could stand it, he stood, arms braced, under the spray letting it pelt his muscles. Rolling his head on his neck he tried to relieve the tension and allowed the water to wet his hair. Pushing away from the tiles, he soaped up and washed before kicking the temperature down to wake him up a bit.

He wasn't tired as such, just worn out and he needed his wits about him when he met the three musketeers. He smiled at that thought—they would be perfect in those roles.

Stepping out of the shower, he dried himself off and changed into jeans and a shirt—he should at least make a bit of an effort—then headed to the kitchen to grab a bottle of water. He opened the bottle, downing half the contents in one go before fishing out his mobile and checking if there were any messages.

Seeing a message from Max, he opened it, swore and checked the time. He'd spent longer in the shower than he realised, meaning he'd have to grab some food at Crush instead.

Max's message stated what he thought of the idea of Sean eating before he left to meet them:

Where the hell are you? You better not blow us off or we'll be heading to your house instead.

Sean shook his head, chuckling to himself as he put his shoes on and grabbed his essentials. Letting himself out the door, he headed to his car, not quite ready for the roasting he knew he would get when he arrived at his destination.

Crush was busy, as to be expected at seven-thirty on a Friday night, but his friends had grabbed a table. *Bonus points for them.*

Sean dropped himself down next to Zak, blowing out a breath. "I'm starved, let's get food," he stated, reaching for the menu.

"Hello and how are you today? I'm fine thank you very much. And you? Yes, I'm good thanks." Ethan cracked up as Max conversed with himself in different voices.

"Shut up. You don't need a hello." Sean smiled as he surveyed the menu.

"Wow, thanks." Max threw a wadded-up napkin at him.

"Stop pretending to be offended, you know it's true," replied Ethan, holding out a fist for Sean to bump. "Hey, Sean, how's things?"

"Good, thanks. What have you been up to lately? I've not seen you around the office much."

Ethan was an architect student who was nearing the end of his first year of work experience at TAC. They had bonded when Sean's mentor had taken on mentoring Ethan too. It meant they spent quite a bit of time together over the course of a week. He was younger than Sean by three years so had three years left at uni with another one-year placement in the middle before he finished his degree.

Sean had chosen TAC for both placements because he found them great to work for, and he'd felt right at home when he'd first walked in the doors. Not every architect student did that. There was a choice of using the same placements or trying different ones to find the best fit.

"No, I've been working alongside Donovan this week. Clive thought it would be good experience to see how other architects work."

"Ah, yes I remember doing that. I was with Clive for most of my first year, but then I was with Nick and Liam, I think it was, for a few weeks. It's definitely worthwhile."

"I'm definitely seeing differences." Ethan laughed. "Donovan is not as…modern, shall we say, as Clive."

Sean laughed. "Yes, I know what you mean. That's probably why Clive has sent you to him though—to show you how not to do the job."

"All right, you two, enough of the work talk." Max interrupted their conversation. "What do you want to order?"

Sean glanced at the menu again and decided on fish and chips. He told Max and handed over some cash to cover that and a soft drink.

Max and Ethan headed to the bar to place the orders, and Zak excused himself to make a phone call. Zak was still in the stage of checking in with his wife from time to time during his nights out. Dane, their son, had just turned one, and Zak was worried that Ashley wasn't coping with their situation. Sean didn't really understand, having never been in that situation before, but he would support Zak as much as he needed it.

As he sat there waiting for the others to return, he tuned in to a conversation being held directly behind him.

"—whether the rumour is true or not, but the app has been hooking teenagers in left, right and centre. They just don't seem to be aware of the dangers involved."

"What type of app is it?" another voice said.

"It's an underground dark app, setting up anonymous hook-ups and providing info on events and stuff to do with BDSM and other dark areas." The man sounded exhausted and pissed off.

"Jesus Christ! That could be a nightmare for teenagers, especially not knowing what they're actually getting themselves into."

"Exactly, hooking up with a complete stranger? Fuck! I can imagine there will be a string of missing people popping up sooner rather than—"

Sean tuned out as Max returned to the table with the drinks; Ethan had apparently gone to the toilet. He wished he had been able to hear more of the conversation, but when Sean turned his head slightly, he saw them getting up from the table and walking to the exit.

"Earth to Sean?" Max bumped his hand to gain his attention. "What's up with you?"

Sean contemplated ignoring the question, but he was curious, and Max might know what it was about— he already knew Max enjoyed BDSM. It was not Sean's thing but each to their own.

"I just overheard someone talking about an app that was going around, making it easy to set up anonymous hook-ups." Sean shrugged. "I was wondering if you knew about it."

Max smirked. "Maybe. What do you want to know for?" Max cocked his head to the side, studying Sean curiously.

"No reason other than I was curious from what I heard." Sean really didn't have any inclination to do anything with an app like that. He was more than happy to find a hook up at a bar.

Max pulled out his mobile and moved over to Sean's side of the table, scooting him over. A few seconds later, he showed Sean an app with a white 'A' and red backwards 'N' on a black filigree background.

"It could be this one. When you log on, you can view information about different events going on in the dark or taboo areas of the world. You can arrange for a hook up and either give away your face when you meet or meet up in a darkened room and be none the wiser afterwards."

"Isn't that dangerous?" Sean would be worried he'd meet a serial killer.

"Not really. Obviously, there is a small chance, but the company who owns it—and, no, I don't know who that is—keeps everything confidential. They know who you are, and you are required to undergo monthly testing, but no one else knows who you are."

"So, if you go missing, I know who to contact?" Sean was completely serious, even though Max laughed at him. He didn't know for definite that Max was using it, but if it was on his phone, he could only guess that he was.

"Yes, you know who to call," he said with a smile.

Sean surveyed Max. "I hope you're careful."

Max's face became serious, and he looked Sean straight in the eye. "Promise I am."

"Promise you are, what?" Zak asked as he took a seat opposite them.

Sean turned away from Max, waiting to hear what he was going to say.

"I promise I'm going to buy the next round."

"Yeah, yeah, promises, promises." Zak laughed.

Ethan came back to the table. "Anyway, what's this I hear about your new love interest, Sean?" The others laughed.

"Fuck you," Sean said without heat. "There is nothing going on regardless of what Max has told you."

"Yes, there is. You spent thirty hours on a project last weekend after barely meeting the guy, then tried to hand the job to someone else, before changing your mind and taking it back." Max smirked. "If that doesn't scream that you have the hots for him, nothing does."

"I do not have the hots for him!"

"So where were you at lunchtime?" Max turned to face him fully, eyebrows raised.

Sean clenched his jaw, annoyed with the direction of this conversation.

"Tell you what, I'll save you. You were meeting with Asher, at the park, with the children he looks after."

Sean gawked at Max in shock. "How did you know that?"

Max grinned. "I went by your office to see you, and your secretary told me you'd gone to see him. And then she said you'd asked for advice what gift to get for three toddlers. It kind of gave you away."

"Shit." Sean shook his head slowly. "Yes, I was there with him. There can't be anything between us, regardless of what happened. He's my client."

"Fuck that!" Ethan threw in. "It doesn't matter if he's your client. Clive married his client!"

"Yeah, I know. But it won't work, he will leave, as they all do." Sean didn't like the tone he'd used, almost petulant and whiny.

"Jesus, Sean. Not everyone will leave. There are some good people around who want the same things as you do." Zak leaned forward on the table, staring Sean in the eyes. "Stability and loyalty. Love. It's not an impossible want."

"I believe it finds you when you need it most," Ethan added.

"What happened between you and Asher?" Max suddenly asked.

Sean blushed and hoped it couldn't be seen in the darkened bar. "He kissed me," he muttered.

"What!" he heard from three directions.

He felt himself flush more. "I went to measure the garage on Monday, and he kissed me while I was there."

"Wow! He's certainly not shy." Ethan chuckled.

"Woohoo! Way to go, Sean." Max elbowed him.

"Enough! Leave me alone," Sean said, outwardly amused by their reaction. "It's not as if I've never been kissed before, you know."

Zak observed him seriously. "But it's the first time you're all tangled up about it. That to me, says it means something." He hesitated. "Even if you're not admitting it."

Sean stared down at his hands. He didn't want Asher to mean something because then, when he left, it would hurt. He would protect himself from that. Even if it cost him his only chance.

CHAPTER EIGHT

ASHER

Asher was so glad it was Saturday. After the night he'd had, he was happy he didn't have to look after any children apart from Janie. She had been up and down all night, which Asher had expected with what day it had been, and he'd had hardly any sleep. She had woken several times with nightmares, and it had taken him an hour or so to coax her back to sleep after each one.

He yawned into his coffee mug, trying to decide whether to cancel his night out or not. He decided not to, firstly because it was only an hour until he was supposed to meet Trent and Logan at the bar, and secondly, he had not been out for a few weeks and seriously needed to destress.

Janie was in her room, sorting out her toys ready to show Jocelyn when she arrived. Jocelyn was Trent's daughter. She was nineteen, at university and had babysat Janie for as long as Asher had cared for her. He didn't go out often, but he allowed himself once or twice a month to go and relax with Trent and Logan, and he definitely needed it this weekend.

Janie came walking into the room, holding two dolls. "Do you think Jo will play babies with me, Uncle Asher?"

Janie had always called her Jo because she had struggled with saying Jocelyn when she was little. "I'm sure she will, sweetheart. You can ask her when she gets here." He glanced at his watch, just as the doorbell rang. "This should be her now."

"Jo! Jo!"

"Hold up, sweetie. Let me open the door first!" He chuckled as he followed in Janie's wake, seeing her bouncing on her toes by the front door.

Asher opened the door, seeing Jocelyn stood there with Trent.

"Hi, Jocelyn, thanks for looking after her." He turned to Trent. "I wasn't expecting to see you. I thought we were meeting at the bar?" He moved out of the doorway to let them in.

"Yeah, I was going to, then I thought I may as well tag along with Jocelyn and see the little pipsqueak before we go." At that, Trent grabbed hold of Janie and swung her up into the air, making her clutch at his arms tight.

"Ahh, Uncle Trent! Let me go!" When Janie had come to live with him, she had automatically called Trent and Logan 'Uncle' whenever they came around. Neither cared, so it stuck.

"Ho-ho-ho, no I can't let a pipsqueak go. She will run away and never be found!"

"Uncle Asher! Jo! Help me!" Janie's squeal could be heard from the kitchen where Trent had 'flown' her to.

Jocelyn laughed. "He never grows up."

"And you wouldn't want him any other way, would you?" Asher watched her, seeing her smile in delight as Trent brought Janie back to them.

Jocelyn shook her head in answer but kept quiet. He wondered why their relationship was so stretched. They both knew the other loved them, but they always refrained from showing or saying it. It seemed a shame to Asher.

"Right, sweetheart. I'm going to leave you in Jocelyn's hands, and I will see you in the morning. Be good for Jocelyn, okay?" Asher knelt to give Janie a hug and kiss before standing and grabbing his things.

"Bye, Uncle Asher." Janie had already turned and grabbed Jocelyn by the hand. "Jo, can you play babies with—" Her voice faded as they walked further into the house.

"Bye, Jocelyn!" shouted Trent, staring after them with a frown. He seemed distracted by something.

Asher would speak to him tonight and see if he could help.

They both exited the house and walked to the taxi that was waiting at the curb. Asher had ordered it earlier, before he'd had second thoughts about going, asking it to be there for six-thirty. It was right on time, as always.

They were dropped off outside Crush and walked into the crowded bar. Crush had become busier and busier over the years they'd been coming, and weekends were always the busiest. Asher would've preferred to come on the quieter days, but he disagreed with drinking alcohol during the week when he had to look after children, so that wasn't possible.

He loved the atmosphere at the bar, the staff were friendly and helpful, there were a wide variety of booths and tables, or stools at the bar to choose from, plus standing room if it was particularly busy. There was even an outdoor area, but it wasn't used very much. He knew the manager, Tom, in passing but only because they had spoken when Tom had served him in the past. He was a constant feature here, as were Charlie, Analise and Rob.

Trent nudged his arm, indicating over the heads of the other patrons to where he could see Logan. They joined him in a booth towards the back of the bar, seeing him already devouring a huge meal.

"Sorry, couldn't wait," Logan said around a mouthful of food.

Asher laughed. "Yeah, I can see that."

"I don't know how you can eat all that and not have a huge stomach!" Trent appeared rather put out about that. They all knew that Trent exercised religiously—being a teacher doesn't always lend a hand to keeping fit, he always said.

"It comes with the job." He smirked as he said it, making Trent scowl at him. Logan was a police officer —Detective Sergeant to be precise—and he was always on his feet, and even though he admitted he had lots of paperwork to complete, he said he made sure to balance it with exercise. They all knew Logan worked hard; his hours were crazy.

Asher studied the menu, though he knew what he would have—the exact same thing he had every time he came here—fish and chips. He replaced the menu, and when Gemma came over, he placed the order with a beer to drink.

"What's happening with you, Trent? You're not your usual bubbly self," Asher asked.

Trent blew out a breath. "I'm having issues with Harper. I went to see her at college the other day because she never answers my calls. Well, we had a right argument, and Harper let loose some comments that I don't think were her own words."

"Like what?" Logan asked.

"Saying I cheated on her mum and that I 'whore' around."

"Jesus! Her mother needs a rude awakening." Asher was furious. He had never liked Trish, but this made him hate her with a vengeance.

Trent shrugged and gazed around the room. "It is what it is. Anyway, Asher, what's going on with your conversion? I know the architect was coming over to see you. Did you get it finalised?" Trent and Logan had both been supportive of his plans, but Trent had taken an interest in the little details surrounding it. Asher wasn't sure whether he was planning on doing something, although that would surprise him given the money situation with his ex-wife. He wasn't going to ignore his questions though. He told them about the first meeting with Sean having gone completely wrong and followed it with the story of finding him skulking around the garage on Monday night and him measuring the inside. He hesitated to tell them anymore but decided he needed fresh ears on this issue.

"And then I kissed him."

It was silent for a minute before Logan and Trent burst out talking at once.

"What the hell!"

"You did what?"

Asher chuckled at their response. He wasn't surprised to be honest. He had never been one to initiate contact with other guys. His last relationship, Matt, had bruised him a little, and he had never had his confidence replaced—he never believed anyone would take a chance on a single guy with a child.

"Yeah, I kissed him," he confirmed.

They both gaped at him as if he was a stranger and he started to squirm under their gaze.

"I like him a lot, okay! He keeps running from me, and it's really beginning to piss me off. I don't know what else to do." To some degree, Asher could understand why Sean kept disappearing, but somehow, he needed to get through to him.

"So, why does he keep running? Has he said anything?" Trent asked.

"Well, he's dropped hints about his parents' death, and he seems really emotionless about it all. I know he has friends but not to what degree he sees them. I honestly think he's scared."

"Sounds like," Logan interjected, "he's closed himself off from people because it hurt too much."

Asher nodded. "That makes sense. So, what do I do?"

Gemma came back with their drinks, and once she had left, Trent rubbed his chin and replied.

"I think you need to get him alone in a public place." Logan laughed, and Asher smiled. "Okay, that sounded stupid, but you get the idea. If he seems to close down when he's alone with you, why not try to talk to him in public where he won't feel so trapped?"

"I have spoken to him at the park yesterday. He still ran from me when things got uncomfortable."

"No, I mean more closed quarters, like on a proper date in a restaurant." Trent leaned forward. "I bet he would feel less inclined to leave you alone in a restaurant that may make you look 'dumped,' for want of a better word. Get him on a date, and he will probably listen to what you have to say."

Asher stared at the table, thoughtfully. "You know, that may work. But how am I going to get him there? I asked him on Monday if I could see him again, and he refused. Twice."

Logan said, "Do you know anyone who might be able to help you? I would love to go through the police route to get some info, but it's not a good idea." He thought for a minute. "Could you pretend to be a client and ask to meet at a restaurant saying you want to get ideas from the place?"

"That could work, but he already knows me." Asher sat up straighter. "I have an idea. I met his friend, Max, the other day. He's an interior designer and is going to quote me on doing the conversion. Maybe I could contact him and ask if he would help me?"

"It's worth a try. The worst thing he could say is no."

"Okay, I'll track Max down tomorrow. I never got his number, but I'm sure he'll have a website or something."

Asher was more confident now he had a plan. He just needed Max's help, and then he might be able to pull it off.

The following day, Asher scoured the internet for Max Hughes' interior design company. It didn't take him long to be honest, but he got distracted viewing his portfolio. He was good. Just from what he'd seen, he knew Max would be the one he wanted on his conversion.

Typing Max's number into his phone, he waited while it dialled. It rang for so long, he thought he would end up with his voicemail, but then a harried, out-of-breath voice came on.

"Max Hughes."

"Hi, Max. Sorry to bother you. I don't know if you remember me from the other day or not? I'm Asher Danvers, we met through Sean Edwards." Asher had absolutely no idea what he was going to say to Max to explain what he needed.

"Hey, yes, I remember. You were setting Sean to rights about the work you wanted done." He heard Max chuckle through the speaker.

"Yeah, sorry about that. It wasn't very professional of me."

"Nah, it's okay. Don't tell Sean this, but he needed to hear what you said."

"He's probably cursing my name right now." Asher paused. "I'm ringing because I wanted to ask a favour. I know you don't know me, but I can't think of any other way to get through to Sean. You're the only person I know who may be able to help me."

"Why? I thought he had agreed to continue with the job?" Max sounded shocked.

"Yes, he has." He blew out a breath. "It's not because of the job. I need…God…I'll be honest with you, Max. I like Sean. A lot. And I want him to give us a chance. So far, everything I have tried has made him run. I was hoping you might be able to help me."

Max was silent for a beat before whistling softly. "I would love to help you, Asher, but Sean is my friend first. I don't think it's a good idea for me to butt in."

"I know you're his friend, and I would never ask you to do anything to put him in danger. I just want…I just want the chance to get him to see what we could be together. That's all. Every time I've tried, he's pushed me away. I really like him, Max." Asher tried to push his point, hoping Max would give in.

After a moment, Max asked, "What's the favour? I'm not saying yes, but I'll hear you out. I'm not making promises."

"That's fine, thank you. I want to try and get him on a date. I'm hoping that he would be less inclined to run from a restaurant full of people, giving me the chance to talk to him."

"That's all well and good. But how are you going to get him there in the first place? If you've already asked him, and he's said no, then it's doubtful he'll back down, even if I put in a good word."

"That is where you come in. I was hoping you would agree to a little white lie." Asher winced. That sounded bad.

"Okay?" Max drew the word out in confusion.

"I want you to tell Sean there is a prospective client who wants to meet him at Romano's tomorrow night. If he asks why at the restaurant, then you could say he wanted to show Sean what he was looking for or something like that." Asher knew it sounded far-fetched, but it just might work.

Max blew out a breath. "I don't know if he will fall for it. He's never had a client stipulate something like that. It might put him off." Max hummed for a moment. "You know about his parents, don't you?"

Asher was thrown by the question. *What did that have to do with anything?* "Um, yes, a little. I know they died in a car accident four years ago."

"Okay, I am going to warn you; Romano's might be difficult for him. It was the last place his parents went before they died." Max carried on before Asher could say anything. "He has been back there before and has been fine. I just wanted to warn you, in case he did, or said, anything strange."

"God! Should I change the place? We could go somewhere else?" Asher didn't want to start the night negatively.

"No, I think that is the best place in all honesty. It will throw him a little off-balance, but it will work in your favour."

"I want us on even ground. I want him comfortable, not off-centre." Asher was ready to cancel the whole thing.

"He will be, but he needs…I shouldn't be saying this. Shit…Okay." Max paused. "Sean needs to be kept off-balance for you to be able to reach him. He's locked his emotions away; he has ever since his parents died. He refuses to let people in, so they don't leave him like his parents did. He has never admitted this out loud, so this is only what I've concluded from my own relationship with him."

"Okay." Asher was apprehensive about the plan now he knew a little more about Sean. He didn't want to scare him away for good. "In your honest opinion, should I do this, Max?"

"Yes, you should. He may hate us for the lies, but someone needs to reach him, Asher. And I think you might be the one to do it."

Asher was silent for a moment, collecting his

thoughts. "All right. So, can you get Sean to Romano's for seven?"

"Sure thing, boss." Max chuckled.

"Thanks. I really do appreciate it."

"No problem."

They said their goodbyes, and Asher sat staring out the back window, second-guessing what he was planning, even though Max agreed it was a good idea. He just hoped Sean would see that, after his initial anger at the situation had waned.

SEAN

"What do you mean, he wants to meet at Romano's?" Max was sitting across from him in his office, looking relaxed as always. "Isn't that a bit weird?"

"No, I don't think so. He said he wants to show you some of the things he likes about the place."

"But I know what the place looks like, why do we have meet there, especially during the evening?" Sean knew he was whining, but he honestly couldn't understand why this guy wanted to meet him there.

"I don't know! I'm just passing on the message. Mr Ashfield said he would be there at seven tonight and that you were welcome to join him to discuss what he wants. That's all I know." Max crossed his ankle over his opposite knee. "I'm sure it wouldn't be a problem if you didn't go. He could find someone else to do it. I just thought you'd like the extra work."

Sean deflated a little at that. Max was trying to be helpful. "Yeah, I know, thanks. It's just short notice, I guess." Sean picked up a folder from his desk and flicked through it, even though he saw nothing.

"What's got you all twisted up?" Max put his foot down and leaned forward.

"Nothing. I'm fine." Sean was not going to tell Max that when he'd said the man's name, his heart had begun to beat a thousand times harder at the 'Ash' part of it. He'd honestly thought Max was trying to set him up with Asher. He was also not going to tell Max that his heart had hurt when he realised it was *not* Asher.

"You learned a new trick since I last saw you?"

Sean gazed at Max in confusion. "What?"

Max indicated the folder Sean had been staring at. "Reading upside down. A new trick?"

Focusing properly, Sean realised he had the paperwork upside down. He shook his head, closing the folder and leaning back in his chair. He didn't know what to say. His mind was going around and around in circles, his heart telling him one thing, his mind another, his instinct yet another. Sean didn't know which way to turn.

He wouldn't admit it to Max though—or any of his friends—because they would see it as a weakness.

Glaring at Max, he denied everything. "I'm fine, just got a lot on. I *will* take this meeting tonight. Thanks for letting me know about it." He glanced at his watch. "I've got to get going. I'll see you later, okay?"

With that, he gathered his briefcase and files, walked out of his office and straight to his car. He didn't have an appointment for another hour, but he could wait there and get a head start on the paperwork.

Four hours later, he was staring at the entrance to Romano's. It had always been difficult for him to enter the place because, although he had never been in here with his parents, this had been their last visit before they'd died.

They had been on their monthly date night when it happened. It was something they had done for as long as he could remember. They always made sure to spend one night a month with each other and no distractions; they said it kept their marriage fresh. And from what Sean could tell, it had worked like a charm.

He had been at his friend's house in Bury St Edmunds, about forty-five minutes away. When he'd got the phone call that they'd been in an accident, he hadn't known what to do. He'd been drinking with

Carl; therefore couldn't drive, but Carl's dad had stepped up and helped. He'd driven him to the hospital —that was the longest trip he'd ever been on—where he'd been taken to an empty room and told to wait. Within fifteen minutes, a doctor had come in to tell him they'd died—a drunk driver had been responsible.

He couldn't remember exactly what happened straight after, all he knew was that he'd cried so much he'd felt empty. By the time he went to see them, he'd felt nothing. He'd filled out the relevant paperwork and then Carl's dad, who had stayed with him, took him home. Carl turned up the next day with his car, which Sean had forgotten about, and then left. Carl had tried calling a few times after that, but Sean hadn't seen him since. After a while, he'd stopped calling too.

As always, people left him. It was what they did. He was better off without anyone.

Regaining his equilibrium, he entered Romano's and asked for Mr Ashfield's table. The waitress took him to the very back of the restaurant, to a table covered in a red tablecloth with a gold runner along the centre. Completing the look were white plates—on top of which was a napkin in the shape of a fan— glasses and cutlery set in front of each seat and a centrepiece of glass bowls with rose petals and floating candles.

Sean raised his eyebrows at the romantic atmosphere but put it down to the restaurant's design.

He lifted his gaze to Mr Ashfield, bracing his hand on the back of the nearest chair when he saw Asher standing from his seat across from him.

"Hello, Sean." Asher stood waiting for a response from him, but he couldn't say anything yet. The waitress obviously realised something was amiss and left them to it, after mumbling something Sean couldn't hear.

"I'm sorry to get you here under false pretences, but I would really like to talk to you properly." Asher indicated the seat opposite him. "Please, sit with me."

Sean glared at Asher, clenching his jaw as anger began bubbling up. He couldn't believe Asher—and Max—had done this to him. He had told Asher several times that he didn't want to pursue a relationship, but he didn't listen. Sean glanced around, noticing a couple of people were staring at them, probably because he had yet to sit down.

He didn't want to cause a scene, so he sat in the chair carefully and studied his plate to calm himself.

The waitress returned. "Good evening. I will be your waitress today. Can I get you some drinks to start with?"

"Would you like some wine, Sean?" Asher's voice penetrated his thoughts.

He glared at Asher, frowning, then smiled at the waitress. "I'd like a Pellegrino, please. Lemon."

"Okay. And for you, sir?"

Sean glanced at Asher, seeing him frowning across at him.

"The same, please," Asher told her.

Sean let out the breath he'd unconsciously been holding. If nothing else, there would be no alcohol to blame for this conversation.

"All right. I will be back in a few minutes with your drinks and to take your order." The waitress walked away.

"Why would I want alcohol, Asher? My parents died in a drunk driving accident." Sean stared at him in anger.

Asher closed his eyes briefly, then seemed to regroup. "You never told me that, Sean," he said quietly.

"I'm surprised Max didn't," he shot back acidly. He glanced out across the restaurant, trying to calm his emotions.

"I'm sorry about this. Truly, I am. If you want me to leave, then just say the words. I would never want you uncomfortable, Sean. I just wanted time to talk with you properly, without all the designs and child-minding getting in the way. That's all."

He glanced across at Asher, seeing sincerity written on his face. Biting his bottom lip, he tried to think what he wanted. He was fine with being there with Asher, he just hated how they went about getting him here. He told Asher the latter.

"I know, and I really am sorry. I just couldn't think of any other way to do it." Asher paused. "Do you want me to leave?"

Sean thought for a moment but knew what he wanted.

"No. We can talk for a bit." Sean could feel the tension leaving his body. He still wasn't happy, but he'd manage to have a civil conversation and some dinner, then tomorrow they'd be back as they were: architect and client.

"Okay," Asher said. "Don't be too hard on Max. He did tell me this wasn't a good idea."

"He still went through with it though, didn't he?" Sean seethed at the reminder; he would be having words with Max the next time he spoke to him. "Anyway, how is the little boy?"

"He's fine, thanks for asking. He's back to making trouble. In fact, the other day, I caught him trying to climb the fence in the back garden." Asher shook his head.

Sean chuckled, and he grabbed the menu. Asher did the same. The waitress brought their drinks over. "Thanks, Rosalia." She smiled in acknowledgement. He took a drink, suddenly realising how thirsty he was. "God, I needed that."

Rosalia smiled. "Have you decided what you would like to order?"

Asher indicated for Sean to order first. "Can I have

the bruschetta for starter, and then pollo milanese for my main course, please?" Sean looked over to Asher.

"Could I have mushroom al forno to start, then roast wrapped salmon, please?"

"No problem, gentlemen. It will be with you shortly." Rosalia retreated, and they replaced their menus.

"Have you been busy today?" Asher asked.

"Fairly. I had an appointment in Peterborough at four, which took nearly an hour, so I hit the traffic coming back in." He reached forward for one of the rose petals from the dish, giving him something to fiddle with. He was a bit unsure what to talk about. "Um, how's Janie?"

Asher huffed out a breath. "She's taken a shine to you, you know. She keeps telling me that when you next come back, you're going to see her bedroom." Asher smiled. "Then she leans forward and whispers, 'Maybe he will play with my dolls.'"

Sean laughed. "She's really bright. I've not been around children much, but she could give some teenagers a run for their money, I'd reckon."

"Definitely. She's four going on forty. She probably has more common sense than I do." Asher paused. "In fact, I guarantee she has."

Sean gazed around the room when the conversation went quiet again. It felt a little uncomfortable, like he should be saying something to fill the gaps, but he wasn't going to push it.

"Can I ask you a question?" Asher's voice interrupted.

He scrutinised him, seeing something in his eyes he couldn't quite decipher. "Sure," he said in hesitation.

"What were your parents like?"

Sean gazed down and fiddled with the rose petal, trying to breathe around the instant lump in his throat. He didn't mind talking about them, and after his outburst earlier, he knew Asher would have questions.

He started small. "They were kind. Gentle. Loving. Everything you could hope for in parents." He snorted and shook his head. "I was a spoiled brat to be honest. I blame it on being an only child and having their undivided attention for twenty-two years. They were always there, no matter what other plans they may have had, if I needed them, they were there." Sean went quiet, lost in the memories.

"What happened?"

"They had been here, actually, for their date night. I didn't know this until after, but CCTV showed them walking to the car park and driving away. They pulled out when their traffic light went green and another car plowed into the side of them. Apparently, the driver had been drinking all day, and the bar he'd been at hadn't taken his keys from him. They said they hadn't seen him leave." Sean grazed his bottom lip with his teeth. "Anyway, Dad died on impact and Mum soon after arriving at the hospital. I didn't get there in time."

Sean studied the rose petal, taking in each tiny detail, trying to take his mind away. He flinched when Asher rested his hand on his arm, squeezing gently.

"I'm sorry for your loss."

Sean nodded and cleared his throat. The emotional rollercoaster was interrupted by Rosalia bringing their food. *Thank God.*

"Thank you," he murmured as the bruschetta was placed in front of him—it smelled divine and his stomach agreed by the sound it made.

Asher chuckled. "I guess you're hungry."

He felt his face go red and inwardly swore that his skin was pale enough to make it noticeable.

They were quiet while they began devouring their starter, only coming back to conversation once their stomachs were slightly satisfied. Sean was the first to break the silence, he was curious about Asher's family.

"So, I know you had a sister. Do you have any other siblings?"

Asher shook his head. "It was just me and Annie. She was six years older than me and gave Mum such grief as a teenager. She was the life of any party. Mum wasn't surprised when Annie announced she was pregnant—she *was* surprised to know that Annie had no idea who the father was."

"Wow."

"Yeah. I have my suspicions that she did know, really, just didn't want Mum to know. Regardless, Janie was born into a family who loved her. What more could we ask for?"

Sean knew Asher would tell Annie's story if he asked, but he didn't think he could handle it. So, he diverted the subject.

"Does your mum live near?"

"Mum lives in Huntingdon now, close to my aunt. We go see her as often as we can, at least once a week."

"What about your dad?"

Asher put his fork on his plate and leaned his arms on the table. "He left before I was born. I've never met him. Have no idea where he is. I know who he is because Mum made sure I knew where I came from. But I've never heard from him and neither has Mum."

"I'm sorry." Sean didn't know what else to say.

"I'm not. As far as I'm concerned, if he didn't want to be there, then it was better he left. Even though it was difficult for Mum, I believe it would have been worse if he'd been there." Asher frowned. "I think he would've been unhappy being there and then maybe taken it out on us. I don't know. It's just a theory after all."

Their situations were so similar in some respects, and so different in others.

CHAPTER NINE

ASHER

He knew Sean had purposefully not asked about Annie's death even though they had talked about Sean's parents earlier. They spent the next few minutes finishing their starters in silence.

Asher couldn't decide whether this date was going well or not, but as far as he was concerned, Sean was still there with him so it was a win. Sean was too quiet though, he needed to find a way to bring him out of his shell a little. Before he had a chance to start a new topic, Rosalia arrived to take their plates.

"Can I get you any more drinks?" she asked.

"Yes, another Pellegrino, please." Sean immediately answered even though his was not quite finished.

Rosalia glanced at Asher. "I'm good, thanks."

"Okay, your mains should be ready in a few

minutes." She stacked the plates in her hands and left them to their conversation.

"What jobs do you have going on at the moment?" Asher leaned forward to make himself closer to Sean. He tried to get Sean to interact with him on a more personal level, but it was difficult. Sean seemed to pull further away every time Asher tried to get near, and he wasn't sure how to reach him except for through his work.

"Well I have this older lady wanting her garage converted into a self-contained unit so her family can stay over to visit." He stopped and chuckled. "Actually, when I was first passed your file, that's what I thought you wanted."

Asher was confused. "Isn't that what I want?"

"Yeah, sorry. I meant I thought you were an older man wanting it converted for family visits. No one had mentioned age, naturally because it doesn't matter to the job, but I concluded from what had been written down about your original phone query that you were an old man." Sean's face was bright red by the time he'd finished his explanation.

Asher laughed. "It's an easy mistake. Hey, I told you at the hospital I was old." He shook his head, chuckling.

"You're not old!" Sean said that a little loud, and then peeked around the restaurant with a grimace. Then he paused and squinted at Asher with narrowed eyes. "I'm denying you're old, but how old are you exactly?"

He laughed again. "I'm thirty."

Sean blew out a breath. "Phew, that was close. See, not old." He nodded as if that was the end of it.

Asher glanced at Sean, smiling at his certainty. "Thanks. So, how old are you?"

Sean grinned. "I'm twenty-seven."

"Ah, a baby."

"Hey, wait, what?" Sean looked indignant. "I've been sticking up for you and you reward me by calling me a baby?"

"You are compared to me."

Sean sat forward. "I may have to rethink my stance on you being old."

Asher's eyes roamed over Sean's face, and as close as he was, he could see the different shades of blue in his eyes and the laughter lines in his face. He must have been silent too long because Sean sat back in his seat and cleared his throat. He realised after a second though, that Rosalia had arrived back with their main courses.

"Enjoy your meals, gentlemen."

Asher studied his plate, not even remembering what he'd ordered until he saw it. He wanted to get back to the fun banter they'd just had.

"So, um, what did you do over the weekend?" He picked up his knife and fork and cut into the salmon.

"Um, I just caught up on some of the jobs I have going on. Watched a little TV. That's it really." Sean's eyes were on his plate, following his actions as he cut up his chicken.

"What do you like to watch?" He placed some salmon in his mouth, groaning at the texture.

Sean was silent for a moment before answering, "Mainly renovation shows, really. I don't watch a lot of TV."

They went silent again.

Asher blew out a breath, resting his cutlery down on his half-finished plate. "Sorry, I'm not normally this bad at conversing." He gave a half-hearted laugh, then leaned forward, resting his arms on the table. "I want to get to know you, Sean, and I'm scared I'm going to push you away instead." He decided to lay it all on the line.

Sean ran his hand through his hair, making it stick up and Asher had to stop himself from reaching forward and brushing it back into place.

"Nothing is going to come of this, Asher. Thank you for your interest, but it's not going to happen. I will never have the kind of relationship that you want." Sean stared at his plate, and he saw him swallow hard.

"Why?" He really did want to know why Sean kept running. "Why do you not want that?"

Sean was silent for so long, Asher thought he wouldn't reply. Sean placed his cutlery on his plate, indicating he was finished and glanced down into his lap. "It's just not for me. I'm happy as I am, Asher. Let's leave it at that." He checked his watch. "I think it's time for me to leave. Thank you for inviting me to dinner."

Asher crooked a smile. "Well, Mr Ashfield is grateful you accepted." He got Rosalia's attention and indicated that he wanted the bill. At her nod, he finished his drink while he waited. She arrived at their table, glancing between the two of them, probably because they were sat in silence.

"Here you go." She went to walk away but Asher called her back.

"Rosalia, I can do this now." He gave her his card and she left to put it through.

"You didn't have to pay, Asher." Sean rested his linked hands on the table in front of him. Asher was surprised he hadn't left already to be honest, but he was grateful for the extra time. He was going to try and walk Sean to his car—there was something he wanted to try.

"It's my treat, Sean. It's the least I can do for getting you here under false pretences."

Sean smiled slightly at that.

Rosalia returned. "Thank you, Asher. I hope you enjoyed your meals. I'm sure we'll see you again soon."

"Thank you, Rosalia. You've been amazing." Asher stood and leaned to kiss Rosalia on her cheek. "Say goodbye to Old Joe for me, please. I didn't get chance to see him tonight."

"I will. Goodnight. And you too, Sean."

"Goodnight, Rosalia." Sean stood and nodded his head to her.

They walked towards the exit, weaving their way between the tables in silence. On the pavement, Asher turned to Sean.

"Where are you parked?" He couldn't see Sean's car, but then it *was* getting dark.

Sean pointed down the street, past Crush. "Down the next street."

"Can I walk you?" Asher tried to keep his voice neutral.

"I don't think—"

"It's not a big deal, unless you make it one, Sean." Asher gazed at him in earnest. "Please."

Sean blew out a breath, staring down the street, then nodded. They both turned to walk towards Sean's car, neither seemed to be in a rush, and Asher was more than happy to stretch it out as long as he could.

As they got to the alley near Crush, Asher decided to make his move. He took a bigger step forward, which took him in front of Sean stopping his progress, then grabbed his wrist, tugging him into the alley.

"What—" was all Sean got out before he was shoved against the wall, and Asher slammed their mouths together. Sean had his hands in between them as if ready to push Asher away. He grabbed them by the wrists and lifted them above Sean's head, holding them tightly against the wall. He ravished Sean's mouth, using all his previous experience to leave them both defenceless. Sean opened his mouth on a gasp, and he used it as an excuse to smooth his tongue alongside Sean's.

Their bodies were pressed tightly together, each of them rolling against the other for any tiny bit of friction they could get. Asher didn't want to let Sean's hands go, even though he was not as tense as before. Asher moved a foot in between Sean's legs, moving them apart a little and allowing himself more room to move.

Sean pulled his head back in a gasp for breath, but Asher wouldn't allow him much. He feared Sean would leave the minute he got his bearings, so taking Max's advice, he tried to keep him off-balance.

Nibbling roughly down the column of Sean's neck, he received a groan of pleasure, which shot straight to his cock. He pressed his lower body closer to Sean's, rubbing against him and elicited a groan of his own. He took Sean's mouth again, the fever heightening. He moved the two wrists into one hand and used his other to grip the back of Sean's neck, holding him closer and moving him where Asher wanted him.

Asher lost track of time as he kissed Sean like he was the missing piece of his life. His heart. He couldn't remember ever feeling like this before, not even with Matt.

He pulled away, softening the kisses until they were separated by a small distance and were breathing each other's air.

Asher asked a question, hoping to catch Sean before he became more aware of their surroundings. "Go on a second date with me? Please?" He kissed Sean's lips with little butterfly kisses, trying to keep him calm. "I'll cook for you."

Sean peered at him with big, pupil-blown eyes that had a hazy lust in them. He licked his lips, which caused Asher to withhold a groan. "Okay." Sean's answer was so quiet, he wasn't sure he'd actually said it, until he repeated it slightly louder. "Okay."

Asher kissed Sean again, this time a lot slower and releasing his wrists so he could wrap his arms around Sean fully. He kept this kiss brief because he was so aroused; he didn't know how much more he could take.

Holding tightly to Sean's hand, he pulled him back out on to the pavement and began the walk to Sean's car. Sean had not said anything so Asher didn't interrupt his thoughts—he was sure Sean would have plenty. Reaching the car, Asher turned towards Sean, planted a kiss on his lips and turned to walk back to his own. He wasn't going to push any more tonight.

He glanced back once, seeing Sean still stood

where he'd left him, staring at Asher. Asher waved then crossed to his own car before getting in and driving away.

SEAN

He rested back against his car, arms by his sides. He didn't quite understand how it had happened, but he'd just agreed to a second date with Asher. He rubbed his hands over his face and around to the back of his neck, then lifted his head to the sky. Thinking about that kiss filled his cock all over again. He hadn't been kissed like that in a long time—probably since his early twenties. When he went for hook ups now, he wasn't bothered about kissing, except for as a means to an end.

He pushed off the car, turned to unlock it and got in. He sat there for a while, trying to figure out what to do. If he was honest with himself, he wanted to go to dinner with Asher. But he knew it wouldn't last so why do it.

He decided to think on it, and he would decide in the morning. He needed to call Asher anyway and sort out finalising the plans—he would cancel the dinner date then if he'd decided to.

When he got home, he wrote himself a note

reminding him to call Max about visiting with Asher tomorrow hopefully. Max could be a buffer for him.

He fell into bed after a shower, thinking he would be awake for hours, mulling over the happenings, but he must have fallen asleep straight away—the next thing he knew, his alarm was blaring at him.

Slapping his hand on the alarm clock, he managed to switch it off after fumbling around a little. He groaned with the thought of moving; he was so comfortable, but he had a full day ahead of him. He turned over onto his back, then remembered last night.

He stared at the ceiling, trying to sort his thoughts until he really had to go shower or he'd be late for work.

By the time he'd arrived at work, he was still none the wiser.

"Morning, Sean." Jessica, TAC's main receptionist, greeted him with a smile, as she did every morning.

"Morning, Jessica. I didn't see you yesterday. Did you have a good weekend?" Sean walked over to collect any messages and post.

"Yes, thanks. Didn't do much except hang out with my kids, so it was quiet for a change." She handed over his items and said a quick goodbye as the phone rang.

"Good morning, Thompson Architect Company. How can I help you?" Jessica's voice was the epitome of professional. Sean waved a goodbye and caught the lift to his floor.

Flicking through his messages, he realised he had one from Asher, from this morning. Reading through it, he blew out a breath in relief, then rolled his eyes at himself. He'd panicked for a moment, thinking Asher would leave a message about their dinner date, but then after reading it, he realised Asher wouldn't do that to him. Asher just wanted to know when Sean could go over to finalise the plans.

Exiting the lift, he walked the short distance to his office and dropped his briefcase on his desk. Deciding to sort it out first, he rang Max to see when he was available for a meeting with Asher.

"Hey, you." Max answered after a couple of rings.

"Don't you 'hey, you' me. You're in big trouble. What the hell were you thinking?" Sean's anger from last night wasn't as sharp this morning, but he still felt mightily annoyed.

"I was trying to help, Sean. I thought it was the right thing to do." He paused. "So, I guess it wasn't?"

Sean tried to corral his thoughts but couldn't get his head and his instinct to agree on anything. He left his heart out of it. "It was okay. Don't get me wrong, I was pissed, but it was nice." Sean cringed at his wording, knowing Max would pounce on it.

"Nice? Well, that could've been worse. I'll take nice." Max laughed. "What's the problem, then?"

"I agreed to a second date." The words were out before Sean realised he was going to say them. What was it with the subject of Asher that everything he didn't want to say just came out anyway?

"Woah! Yeah! Second date. Well done, Sean." Max whistled.

"Shut up, Max. I was ringing because I need to go around to Asher's house to finalise plans and wanted to know if you wanted to come to put your own opinions on the plans."

"Ah, you want me to be the buffer." Max was far too clever for his own good, but Sean denied it anyway.

"No. I'm asking for the exact reasons I said." He rested his head in one hand. "If you don't want to come, that's fine."

"Nah, I'll be there. Would love to see you two inter-acting again. Last time was a doozy." He laughed long and hard at that.

"Very funny. What time are you free?"

"Today? Um, I've nothing unless you want to make it this evening? I can do six-thirty?" Sean could hear paper rustling; he could imagine Max rifling through his diary.

"Let me check with Asher, and I'll ring you back."

"Okay, I'll be here."

"Well, where else are you going to go?" Sean didn't wait for a response and just rang off.

He immediately dialled Asher's number. He answered surprisingly quickly.

"Asher, it's Sean." He tried to keep his voice neutral

but was sure he failed. He kept seeing Asher pressed up against him in the alley.

"Hi." Asher sounded surprised. Maybe he thought Sean wouldn't call back. "I didn't expect you to ring back so quickly."

"Yeah, I, um, just talked to Max and thought the both of us could come over to finalise the plans. Max might be able to give you some other ideas about the layout you want."

"Sure, when were you thinking? Hold on a sec, Sean." He heard a noise on the other side of the phone and muffled voices before Asher came back. "Sorry, Cooper was asking for some juice."

"That's okay. Um, if you want sooner rather than later, Max can do six-thirty tonight?"

"Erm, yeah okay. I can do that."

"You sure you're not busy? Or too tired?" Sean didn't know why he was asking those questions.

"Nah, it's fine. I'll see you at six-thirty, then."

"All right. See you later."

"Bye." It was a good job Asher put the phone down because Sean didn't think he would have been able to.

He paused for a minute to collect his thoughts, then called Max back.

"Yeah?"

"Six-thirty tonight is fine. I'll text you the address and meet you there."

"Why can't you pick me up?"

"Because you're a lazy sod, you can drive yourself. See you later." Sean hung up the phone to Max's laughter and shot off a text with Asher's address.

Leaning back in his chair, he stared at his computer. He needed to focus now; otherwise, he'd get nothing done—again.

CHAPTER TEN

ASHER

Asher was glad he didn't have to wait several days to see Sean again. Yeah, okay he was bringing Max with him, but at least he'd get to see him. After last night, he'd expected Sean to disappear and do everything through email and messages.

He'd decided to ask Jocelyn to babysit for a couple of hours so he wouldn't be distracted by Janie. He could focus on Sean—on the plans—without issue.

All the children had left by six, so he had a little time to clean up the house ready for tomorrow. Jocelyn arrived on time and went off to find Janie who was in her room reading. Asher painstakingly waited for the doorbell to ring, and even though he was expecting it, he still jumped.

He almost ran to the door, then paused before opening it to make sure he didn't seem too eager. He shook his head at himself, he'd reverted to teenager mode.

Opening the door, his eyes immediately went to Sean, drinking in the sight of him in jeans, a white t-shirt and a black leather jacket.

"Hi, come on in." He managed to take a step back to welcome them into his home. In his periphery, he saw Max walk in, but his gaze was on Sean—who appeared very uncomfortable. That wouldn't do. He turned to Max and held out his hand. "Nice to see you again, Max. Let's head to the kitchen and I'll make some coffee." He led the way, hearing Sean tell Max about Zak's woodwork.

Stopping in front of the kettle, Asher turned and asked if they wanted tea or coffee.

"Coffee, please. White, no sugar," Max replied with a small smile.

"I'm good, thanks." Sean sat at the table, placing a folder in front of him.

"I have water or juice if you want something cold." Asher opened the fridge ready for whatever Sean wanted.

"Um, water's good then, please."

He grabbed a bottle of chilled water and set it in front of Sean, wishing he would meet his gaze—Sean was having none of it though. Asher glanced at Max and saw his gaze on them both, smirking. He had a sinking feeling Max knew what had happened between them—why else would he have looked at him like that?

He turned back to the coffee machine and finished the drinks. Setting Max's in front of him, and receiving thanks, he fetched the folder Sean had left with him and brought it to the table.

"I've gone through the designs you gave me, and I've marked the bits I like most on each." Asher passed the plans over to Sean, seeing Max move closer to look.

Sean opened the folder and spread the three designs out on the table. Max whistled and glanced at Sean.

"These are fantastic, Sean. You haven't made designs like this in a while." Max pulled one closer to him.

Asher frowned at Max, then glanced toward Sean, seeing him glance up at him then back down, blushing.

"Enough, Max." Sean's voice was quiet but firm.

"Why? These designs are amazing! I can understand why they took you so long now. You haven't made one like this since I first met you."

"Enough!"

Max seemed to realise Sean was serious and stopped talking, but he peered at Asher and smirked. Asher wasn't sure why Max thought these designs were anything special—he knew *he* thought they were, but Max seemed to be trying to make a point. He'd never requested an architect before; he wasn't sure if there were different types, so he was a complete novice. He wouldn't make Sean more uncomfortable by asking.

Sean began talking to Max, pointing things out on the designs. Some of it went over Asher's head, but he got the gist of what they were saying. He was amazed by the transformation in Sean every time he talked about architecture and design. He became confident, eager and a little manic.

"Can I have a look at the space, Asher?" Max asked.

Asher nodded and rose to get the keys. He led the way out the back door. After unlocking the garage, he switched the lights on and moved to the side so Sean and Max could enter.

They both moved further into the space, pointing at the walls, consulting the plans, occasionally one of them wrote something down. They both went into the garden and inspected the outside of the garage, talking about pipes and waste lines. After about fifteen minutes of this, they walked back into the garage and called him over.

"So, how about we do this?" Sean explained that because of where the pipes lay, the kitchen would be best situated on the wall nearest the house. "You would still be able to keep this back door to get into the garden, although we will replace it with a sturdier one. To the front of the kitchen area, we could put a doorway in from the driveway, allowing an entry point for parents, which you asked for. The rest of the wall could have a large window and then another window to the front of the garage, where the double doors are presently." Sean was using his hands to create his ideas in the air. "The pipes for the shower and toilet will be easier to extend so they could both sit in the far corner. It will allow a large open space area in the centre for you to use."

"And what I would suggest is to have some low storage units as well as a couple of full height ones. It will provide lots of space to store toys and games and other stuff but still allow you to have floor space." Max described his thoughts on the interior design. "If you wanted to split the area up a bit, you could use some moveable storage for if you want to have a change around. Otherwise, you could just use tables to do it. Have you decided on what kind of furniture you wanted in here?"

Asher was blown away by the insight of them both. Sean had managed to get the garage sounding light and open, and Max had taken his needs as a child-minder into account when explaining about storage. He was overwhelmed.

He cleared his throat. "Um, I know I want a sofa and TV so the older kids can relax. And I need some tables for crafts and a dining table with chairs. Apart from that I was thinking about bean bags or something like that for the little ones to sit on."

Max nodded. "Okay, I can work with that. What else do you see?" At Asher's raised eyebrow, he laughed and said, "This is your building, Asher. You need to tell me what you want, and I can try and get it to look like that for you."

He blew out a breath. "All right." He thought for a moment. "I want a reading corner—not too many books but enough for a variety of choices—with some material that makes it…kind of appear secluded, not completely separate but can take you away from the rest of the room." Max nodded. "I'd also like somewhere I can put notices for the parents and somewhere for the children's artwork. And maybe having something on the floor that's easy to clean for the craft areas?"

"Okay, I can see that. Anything else?"

Asher surveyed the space, trying to imagine what he wanted it to look like. "Apart from somewhere for them to put their coats, bags and shoes, and then wellies, etc, I can't think of anything else."

Max examined his notes, tapping his pen on the page. "Yep, that's definitely doable. Let me get some ideas together, and I will get something over to you."

"Thanks."

"Okay, I think we're sorted then," Sean said as he began to make his way out of the garage. "I'll get the final plans to you by next week so you can double check everything is how you want it. Then we'll go from there."

They entered the kitchen to the smell of something sweet. Jocelyn and Janie were at the counter, bringing out a batch of cookies.

"Mmm, they smell good." Asher went close trying to pinch one, but Janie shouted at him.

"No, Uncle Asher! These are for Sean and… and…" She stared over at Max. "Um…Uncle Asher? What's his name again?" she whispered as only a child could—loudly.

"My name is Max, sweetheart. What's yours?" Max went over to Janie and kissed the back of her hand like a princess. Janie's smile grew as wide as her eyes.

"I'm Janie."

"Nice to meet you, Janie."

"Do you want a cookie?" Janie asked.

"That would be lovely, thank you." Max reached over and grabbed one, throwing it from hand to hand when he realised they were hot. "Ooh, hot, hot!"

"And that, Janie, is why we don't touch the cookies until they've cooled," Jocelyn said as she put the oven gloves on the counter. "If you're back, Asher, I'll head off if that's okay?"

"Of course, thanks so much for coming on short notice." Asher came around the counter and followed Jocelyn to the hallway. She grabbed her belongings.

"That's okay. Janie's a sweetheart."

Asher pulled out his wallet and paid Jocelyn for her time and saw she got into her car before shutting the door and heading back to the kitchen. He entered the kitchen to find Janie bracketed by Sean and Max, and they were all decorating the cookies.

He leaned against the doorway, watching them laughing and nudging each other. "What are you—" he began before he heard a knock at the door. "Hold that thought." He walked back to the front door.

Jocelyn was stood there, smiling up at him. "Sorry, Asher, my car won't start. It was playing up the other day and Dad checked it over saying he thought it sounded like the gears. I'm taking it to the garage this weekend. Can I wait here until Dad gets here? He's on his way."

"Of course, come on in. I don't know anything about cars; otherwise, I would try to help." They walked towards the kitchen. "These lot are decorating the cookies you made," he said as they entered.

"I can see that!" Jocelyn laughed as they watched the boys make a mess of the cookies. Janie, however, was doing a good job.

They sat around the kitchen table with coffees, juice and cookies until they heard another knock at the door, then a bellowed, "Anyone here?"

"In the kitchen!" Asher shouted back.

Trent strode into the room, stopping when he saw

how many people were there. Or at least Asher assumed that was why. It wasn't very often Asher had people around who weren't Trent or Logan.

"Hi," Trent said slowly.

"Hi, Uncle Trent," Janie replied, eating her way through the cookie she was supposed to be decorating.

"Hey, Trent. How are you?" Asher rose and headed to the coffee pot. "Do you want a drink before you go?"

"Best not. I think Jocelyn needs to get back for her studying. Or do I have time for a coffee?" Asher realised the last question was aimed at Jocelyn.

"If you want a coffee, you can have one," Jocelyn said, looking her phone.

Trent stared at her for a moment, then turned to Asher and shook his head. "Nah, it's okay, Asher. I'll get her home. Thanks."

"No problem."

"Is it okay to leave her car here, and I'll get it sorted tomorrow? It's a bit late now," Trent asked.

"Of course. There's plenty of room on the drive," Asher replied.

"Thanks." Trent glanced over at Sean and Max, then back at Asher, eyebrows raised.

"Sorry, I'm being rude. Trent, this is Sean Edwards, the architect I told you about." Asher hoped Trent wouldn't say anything to that descriptive, and he didn't thankfully, but Asher could see understanding dawn in his eyes. "And this is Max Hughes, the interior designer. Guys, this is Trent Walker. I used to work with him at the primary school."

"Hi, Trent, nice to meet you." Max rose from his chair, hand outstretched towards Trent.

"Yeah, you too. And you, Sean."

"Hey, Trent." Sean was quiet, watching the interaction between Max and Trent. Asher studied them again, realising they hadn't let their hands drop.

"Dad, do you mind if we head out?" Jocelyn's voice seemed to shock everyone back into motion, and Max and Trent jumped apart.

"Um, sure. Yeah, let's go." Trent turned to Asher. "I'll catch up with you soon. Bye, pipsqueak."

"Bye, Uncle Trent. Bye, Jocelyn." Janie gave an icing-covered wave.

"Bye. Thanks again, Jocelyn."

"No problem, see you later."

Trent and Jocelyn headed out of the kitchen, and Asher returned to his seat, only to get up again when Sean stood.

"We best be heading off as well. Thanks for the cookie, Janie."

"Do you have to go now, Sean?" Janie asked with her puppy dog look.

Sean hesitated but nodded. "Yeah, I do, Janie. But I'll come back another day."

"You have to. You haven't seen my bedroom yet!" Janie exclaimed.

Sean smiled and rubbed his hand against her cheek. "I'll be back soon."

Janie jumped up from her seat and threw her arms around Sean's legs. *No doubt covering him in icing*, Asher thought. Then she turned and did the same to Max, only he got a proper hug because he was still sitting down.

"Thank you for the cookie, sweetheart." Max hugged her back then stood to leave. "Thank you for the coffee. It was sorely needed." Max laughed.

Asher responded in kind. "No problem. Thanks for coming around."

"I'll get the plans to you asap, Asher." Sean glanced at him before heading to the hallway. He paused for Max to catch up and opened the front door, waving and closing the door behind him.

Asher stood staring at the door, just like last time, but today his time was cut short because Janie interrupted him.

"Uncle Asher, I made a bit of a mess," she whispered.

Asher gazed at her, smiling. "Let's go tidy up, sweetheart."

SEAN

Sean was parked outside of Asher's house, two days later, trying to get the courage to go to the door. He'd received a text message from Asher the day before, short and simple.

My house. Five-thirty. Thursday.

He'd viewed the message for a long time, trying to decide what to do. He knew he had already agreed to go on a second date, but he was struggling to keep himself away from them as it was. He didn't think this would help any.

As he watched, the front door opened, and Asher stood there, leaning against the doorframe. He didn't beckon Sean in or do anything other than wait and study him. It calmed him a little to know that Asher was not pushy, at least in some things. He sat for a few more minutes, then got out and walked towards the house.

By the time he got there, he was breathing heavier than usual, the stress of his decision weighing on him. Stopping in front of Asher, he smiled, hoping he appeared confident.

"Sean." Asher smiled as he spoke his name softly. Asher reached forward slowly, resting a hand on his shoulder and smoothing it down his arm to link their fingers together. Sean glanced down at their joined hands, breathing heavier still. He felt panic begin to set in and the fight or flight response awakening, but just a squeeze from Asher's hand made it disappear, and Sean breathed easier.

Pretending nothing was amiss, Sean gazed at Asher again. "Are you going to invite me in?"

Asher nodded. "I was waiting for you to decide you *wanted* to come in." He smiled and moved aside so Sean could enter without letting go of his hand.

"I won't deny that it's not an easy decision, but I'm here as I said I would be."

That earned another squeeze of his hand, and he felt his body relax marginally.

"Well, I said I was going to cook for you, so I have. But I forgot to ask if you were allergic to anything, so I'm hoping that what I've made is all right."

"And what's that?" Sean asked.

"Lasagne with garlic bread and salad."

"It sounds delicious. And to answer your concern, I'm not allergic to anything." They walked towards the kitchen, and Asher deposited Sean on a stool at the counter before turning to walk away. Between one heartbeat and the next, Asher was back with his lips hovering over Sean's.

"I don't want to ask, but this time I will. Can I kiss you?" Asher's words were spoken into Sean's mouth but without any contact.

Sean felt himself leaning forward in answer, and their lips connected briefly several times before Asher pulled back.

"Thank you." With that, he turned and walked to the oven.

Sean sat there barely breathing, eyes on Asher as he pottered around the kitchen, finishing up their dinner. He jumped when he felt a hand on his shoulder and realised Asher was standing next to him.

"Breathe, Sean, breathe. Come on, you'll pass out if you don't breathe for me." Asher's hand travelled to the back of Sean's neck, and he felt him pushing down as if to put his head between his legs. That snapped him out of his head, and he let out a huge sigh and took a deep breath, several times.

"Jesus, Sean. You scared the shit out of me." Asher wiped a hand over his face and blew out a breath. "No more kisses for you if that's how you respond." He chuckled.

Sean heard himself whimper and hoped it had been quiet enough that Asher didn't hear, but glancing at his face, he realised it hadn't. The heat and longing in Asher's eyes were overwhelming, so he turned away.

"Okay, dinner." Asher gave his neck a squeeze—Sean only realised then he still had hold of him—and went back to the food.

Sean removed his suit jacket but continued to watch Asher until a steaming plate was placed in front of him. Another was placed to his right, followed by two sets of cutlery.

"It smells amazing, Asher, thank you." Sean finally found his voice.

"You're welcome." Asher placed two bottles of Pellegrino on the table within reach before sitting down. "Dig in."

"I've just realised—where's Janie?" he asked.

"At Martine's for the night. A spa night apparently."

Sean chuckled. "I'm sure she'll enjoy that."

He began eating the dinner as Asher talked about his day looking after Janie, Enrico and Laney. It was only after he'd finished his food and drink that it occurred to him Asher was trying to make him feel comfortable.

Once they had both had their fill, Asher tidied the plates up and placed a dessert on the table.

"Now, I made this for tonight, but you have a choice to make." Asher smiled at him. "We can eat some now, then go watch a movie or something. Or we can go watch a movie now and eat some later."

The apple crumble and custard smelled delicious, but Sean had to listen to his stomach. "Dessert later. My stomach needs a break," he said with a self-conscious laugh.

"Yeah, mine too." He covered the dessert with a net. "Come on, let's go raid the movie cupboard."

"Oh, come on, haven't you got on-demand yet?" Sean joked, picking up his suit jacket, and followed him into the lounge, placing the jacket on the side of a chair.

"Yes, I have, for your information," Asher replied with a glance over his shoulder and a smirk, "but I thought you might like to see what movies I love best. That way we can debate the intricacies of sci-fi versus action, or whatever."

Asher went over to a large unit in the corner and opened both doors, making visible a huge selection of DVDs. The bottom shelves were—he presumed—all Janie's, unless Asher had a fetish for princesses Sean hadn't yet realised. He smiled behind Asher's back, making sure it didn't show when Asher turned around.

Sean was amazed by the variety he saw. There must have been hundreds of DVDs, and they covered every possible genre: sci-fi, action, horror—*no, thank you*—comedy, thriller, fantasy and even romance. He inspected them all; there was no way he could choose. Sean glanced around to Asher and shrugged.

"I have no idea."

Asher laughed and shook his head. "Want me to choose?"

He nodded.

"Okay, well give me a clue then. What type of films do you like?" Asher swapped places with Sean and proceeded to look through his own collection.

"Um, anything but horror. I do have an affinity for action or fantasy." Sean went and sat on the sofa, making himself comfortable.

"Okay…" Asher hummed his way through them as Sean watched him. Sean saw the play of the muscles in his back as he moved his arms or leaned forward, he couldn't take his eyes away. Asher was a fine specimen, and if Asher hadn't been wanting more than one night, Sean would've happily taken him to bed immediately.

"Ah, got it." Asher produced a DVD case and, making sure to hide it from Sean's view, moved over to the cabinet holding the electrical equipment. After putting in the DVD, Asher sat himself down on the sofa next to Sean with the remotes in his hand.

"So, what are we watching?" Sean asked to take his mind away from other thoughts.

"You'll see." Asher smirked as he got the film up and running.

A few minutes later, *Dragonheart* started, much to Sean's surprise.

"I love this film." Asher pronounced, settling himself down before sitting up again. "I forgot our drinks. Back in a minute." Asher disappeared, then returned with four bottles of water. Placing them on the table, he dropped down again and lifted his sock covered feet to the coffee table. "If you want to put your feet up you can, just take your shoes off first."

Sean was spellbound by Asher's feet. He hadn't noticed he only wore socks but now he could see his long narrow feet crossed at the ankles. Sean was frozen in indecision before he took a breath and leaned forward. He removed his shoes, placing them under the table out of the way, and lifted his feet alongside Asher's.

They were both rested in identical positions, heads against the back of the sofa, hands on their stomachs and ankles crossed on the coffee table. If Sean wasn't so anxious, he would have laughed.

The film began, and they got lost in the story, making comments throughout. To Sean, it felt like the film went by fast. He hadn't realised how much fun it was to just sit and talk about something random.

"Right, your choice now." Asher nudged Sean's feet with his own and indicated to the cupboard. "I'll get dessert while you choose. Don't take forever."

After scanning through some, he decided on *Guardians of the Galaxy*. He was trying to figure out how to work Asher's system when a warm body pressed up behind him. Sean stiffened slightly and not just his frame. He closed his eyes as Asher reached his arms either side of him and put the disc in. He didn't move straight away.

Sean felt Asher rest his head on his shoulder, and then run his nose up the side of Sean's neck before reaching his ear. As Asher took his earlobe into his mouth and sucked gently, Sean's head fell backward against Asher's shoulder. He felt Asher's arms come across his chest and waist, pulling him closer. All Sean could do was feel as Asher's lips and teeth tantalised his ears and neck.

Sean had no idea how long they stayed like that, but Asher's voice broke into his high.

"Let's watch the movie," Asher whispered in his ear, but he didn't move until Sean nodded and put his full weight back on his own two feet. Blushing as they drew apart, Sean went and sat down again, eyes on his lap.

"Don't leave me now, Sean. I have crumble and custard." Asher swung a wooden spoon about as if to fend off enemies.

Sean couldn't help but laugh. "Give me my dessert, evil one."

Asher threw himself on the sofa, then reached forward for the bowls and spoons. "Your wish is my command, kind sir."

Sean dug in as Asher started the movie, and soon, they were back to the camaraderie they had previously, although the heat of their encounter had not dimmed. He was aware of every move Asher made which was a little disconcerting for him.

About half an hour into the movie, after dessert had been demolished, Sean had found Asher was sitting closer than before—or Sean was sitting closer to

Asher. He didn't know, but they were touching all down one side. A few minutes later, Sean felt Asher take his hand and link their fingers, like he had done when Sean had arrived earlier that evening.

It felt comforting, so Sean didn't protest and continued watching the movie. A little while later, he realised Asher was resting his head on his shoulder, his hair tickling Sean's neck. He had no idea when he'd done it, but there it was. He tried to figure out how to react and realised he didn't need to; he was content.

During a fight scene, Asher turned his face into Sean's neck, nuzzling his nose against his warm skin. Sean tilted his head to the side to allow Asher more room. At that movement, Asher twisted to his side, smoothing his free hand upwards over Sean's chest to cup his face as Asher found his lips.

Sean opened for him immediately and closed his eyes against the sensations—lips against lips, hands entwined, hand against neck, hand in hair. He realised he'd grasped Asher's hair and was running his hands through it. Then Asher let go of his hand and pushed himself up, allowing him to turn Sean and lower him to the sofa.

Sean startled at the movement but was soon lost in Asher's lips. Asher licked inside his mouth, sliding along his tongue before following the curve of the roof of his mouth back out again. Sean's tongue chased, and Asher sucked on it hard, deepening the kiss until they struggled to breathe and had to stop for air.

Panting into each other's mouths, they kept eye contact as their hands roamed over their bodies. Asher's fingers reached for Sean's shirt buttons, hesitating for a moment, then undoing the first one.

Sean was more than happy to remove a few layers, so let Asher do his thing, then when he was halfway, Sean started on Asher's shirt. He noticed belatedly that Asher's shirt was the same colour as his eyes, then forgot the thought when Asher came in for another kiss.

He lost all thought as Asher devoured him, his fingers losing the fight with the buttons and just holding on for dear life. Their lower bodies were pressed tightly together, their minute movements more tease than relief.

Sean moved his head to the side to breathe again, and Asher carried his kisses down his body. His shirt was now fully open, and Asher had the whole of his torso to explore. Sean made quick work of the remainder of Asher's buttons before pushing it off his shoulders and following it down the length of his arms, feeling the mass of muscles as he went.

Sean arched when Asher licked his nipple then circled it several times before sucking it into his mouth with strong pulls. He felt arcs of pleasure streak down to his cock, which was harder than he'd ever remembered it being.

He wrapped his arms around Asher's head once he started on the other nipple, still playing with the first with his fingers. Sean widened his legs to get more friction on his lower body, making Asher shift position. Sean's cock was now nestled against Asher's chest, and he used it shamelessly.

His cock was so hard, the zipper of his trousers hurt, so he removed a hand from Asher's hair and slid it to his button. Flicking it open had Asher stopping to see what he was doing, then his eyes met Sean's with a smirk, and he began to move down.

The relief he felt at having his cock less confined was short lived. Asher undid his trousers completely, pulling them down his legs and off along with his socks before doing the same with his underwear.

Sean was naked, and Asher was not quite. Asher didn't give him a chance to rectify that because he dove right back to where he had been—kissing his way down Sean's stomach.

Sean felt like all his nerve endings were electrified and every touch tingled, no matter how hard or soft. When Asher grasped his cock in his hands, Sean bucked his hips. "Fuck, Asher!"

"Soon, baby. Soon." With that, he engulfed Sean's cock completely, taking him in as far as possible. When he pulled back, he placed his hand at the base of his cock and used his tongue to lick around his hood before taking him in again. This time, as he rose his hand moved up with him and led the way down again, mouth surrounding Sean in wet heat.

"God! That feels good." Sean was panting hard, fingers wrapped around the sofa cushions below him. He couldn't take his eyes off Asher's head, mesmerised by the up and down motion.

Asher pulled off completely, leaning his head down to tongue his balls, then trace his tongue up the whole length of his cock, playing close attention to the sensitive area each time he reached the top. He repeated this several times until Sean couldn't cope anymore and bucked up, seeking heat.

Asher locked eyes with him and took the tip of Sean's cock into his mouth. He kept his head still, but his tongue was devastating him, flicking over and over the sensitive nerve bundle. Sean bucked again, and Asher swallowed him down, keeping him in his throat for several seconds.

"Shit! Fuck!" Sean couldn't gather any other words.

Lifting off, Asher gasped in air before repeating the action. The second time he pulled off, he rested the side of his face against Sean's thigh and used his hand to jerk him roughly.

"Ah! God, Asher!"

Asher leaned forward again and consumed his cock

once more, hands and mouth working in tandem to make Sean crazy.

"Fuck! Asher, stop, I'm going to come!" Sean threw his head back against the cushion, trying to hold on to his sanity.

Asher lifted off. "Let go," he said before returning to what he was doing. He, again, rested the hood of Sean's cock just inside his mouth and let his tongue do its magic.

Sean gripped the cushions tightly as he felt his muscles contracting in readiness. "Fuck, fuck, fuck!" Sean surged against Asher's mouth. "I'm coming! Fuck!" He felt the climax begin as his muscles became so rigid, he could hardly move. He was immobilised by the force of his orgasm, unaware of his surroundings. He came to when a mouth descended onto his, gently and without force. He opened in invitation and received little licks as a reward. Sighing, he opened his eyes and stared into Asher's, whose were bright, and passion filled.

CHAPTER ELEVEN

ASHER

"That was gorgeous. *You* were gorgeous," Asher whispered to him before kissing him again.

Sean blushed, though why, Asher didn't know, especially after what they just did. Sean reached for his shoulders, pulling him down fully on top of him. Asher could feel his cock, still confined within his jeans, hard as a rock against Sean's stomach. Sean pushed Asher back again and reached a hand down, undoing them to free his cock, which made Asher groan and drop his head on Sean's shoulder.

Sean pushed Asher's jeans down as far as he could, then used his feet to push them until they were completely off. He made Asher spread his legs by placing them on the outside of his own.

Sean ran one hand from Asher's shoulder, down his back to his ass, squeezing gently. Sean's other hand leisurely made its way down his chest, plucking at his nipples as he went. Having his arms bracketing Sean made Asher feel like they were in their own little bubble—no one could touch them here, it was just the two of them.

Sean stroked his hands further south, setting Asher's arms visibly trembling, and he realised he may not be able to stay in this position long. Wrapping his hand around Asher's cock, Sean pumped up and down several times. Asher noticed distantly that Sean couldn't keep his eyes off what he was doing, and neither could Asher. The vision of his cock emerging through Sean's fist was hot.

"Fuck! Oh, god!"

Sean reached his other hand further between his cheeks, resting his fingertip against his hole, which made him buck forward. Sean added a little pressure, not penetrating him but so Asher felt it when he began making small circles against his hole.

"Ah, oh, fuck!" The pleasure was immense.

Keeping up the motion of both hands had Asher squirming, arms shaking even more.

"Fuck, Sean. I can't hold off much more." Asher's voice was gritty and hoarse and felt like a desert.

Sean tightened his grip and moved faster, twisting a little at the top, and then firmly pressed the finger he had against Asher's hole, penetrating with just his fingertip.

"Ah! Ah!" Asher moved his hips in time with Sean's motions, his eyes still on the vision before him. As Sean next reached the tip, he slid his palm across the head, before gripping and pumping again.

"Shit, shit! Fuck! Sean!" Asher couldn't stop moving now, fucking himself into Sean's palm and onto his finger. "I'm coming! Fuck, Sean!"

His pure white come landed on Sean's stomach, giving Asher a sense of ownership as he marked Sean, the idea making him horny all over again. Asher's arms finally gave way, and he rested on top of Sean, breathing heavily into his neck. Sean rested his arms against Asher's back, stroking up and down his spine.

They lay there for several minutes before Asher made to move. He pulled back, smiling at Sean. "Thank you." Asher leaned down to kiss him, softly.

Asher stood, holding Sean's hands to pull him up with him and, keeping hold of one hand, led him up the stairs.

They entered a master bathroom suite which was a huge, completely tiled splash room. It had a huge claw-footed bath, a double sink, a toilet, and a several-person sized shower area with a drain in the centre of the room.

Asher let go of his hand to turn the shower on, then indicated for Sean to go first. He walked towards the shower, eyes wide, then groaned in delight as the shower sprays hit him from all sides.

Asher chuckled again. He had designed this bath-room just how he wanted it. It was one of the first things he'd had done when he moved in.

Asher closed in behind Sean, then wrapped his arms around his waist, resting his head on Sean's shoulder.

"I enjoyed myself tonight. Thank you for coming over." Asher turned his head to kiss below his ear before turning Sean around and reaching over to get the shower gel. He soaped his hands and washed Sean from head to foot, then pushed him back into the water to wash it off.

Asher swapped their positions and began to wash himself, but Sean ran his soapy hands over Asher's body, careful to wash every inch of him.

When they'd finished, Asher switched off the shower and headed over to the heated towel rail, throwing a towel over to Sean. Sean was staring at the towel, looking deep in thought.

"You okay?" Asher asked, towelling his hair.

Sean nodded, drying himself thoroughly, then paused.

Asher realised he'd probably just remembered his clothes were downstairs. He went over to him and wrapped his arms around his waist.

Kissing him lightly, Asher whispered, "Stay with me?"

At those three words, Sean flinched, and Asher's

heart sank. He knew what Sean was going to say before the words had even left his mouth. "Sorry, I have to get going." He didn't make an excuse, he just pulled out of Asher's arms, wrapped the towel around his waist and went downstairs.

By the time Asher entered the lounge dressed in joggers and a t-shirt, Sean was dressed and had his shoes on, jacket held in his hand.

"Thanks for a great night, Asher," he said, and he strode towards the front door.

"You running again?" Asher called to him. But Sean didn't reply, he just let himself out.

Asher slumped down onto the sofa, resting his head in his hands. He heard a car start then the engine noise getting quieter as the car drove away. He honestly felt like crying. He thought he'd finally got through to Sean, but then he'd gone and left.

He blew out a breath and reached for the remote. Sitting back again, he flicked through the channels to see if there was something that would take his mind of Sean.

He settled in when he found a horror movie. *I doubt I'll root for the victims tonight, especially with the mood I'm in now.* Knowing Sean didn't like them made it easier to forget—for a while, anyway.

SEAN

Sean arrived at Crush without even realising it had been his destination. He parked his car and went inside, not caring about his appearance. He chose a stool at the bar, receiving the attention of the bartender straight away.

"What can I get you?" the bartender said as he wiped the counter in front of him, probably out of habit more than the need to clean it.

"Bourbon on the rocks, please. And keep them coming." He kept his voice quiet even though the bar was quite loud. He blew out a breath as he sat and linked his fingers together in front of him. Staring down at his hands, he thought about what had happened that night.

He hadn't meant to let it go as far as it did. *But I did want him*, he finally admitted to himself.

"I have an ear should you need it." A voice brought him out of his melancholy. The bartender was back, having placed the drink in front of him.

"Huh?" Sean said, blankly, then realising what the bartender had said, replied, "Uh, thanks. I'll keep that in mind."

Without second guessing his stance on alcohol, he threw back the drink in one go, feeling it scorch his throat—a familiar and unfamiliar feeling all at once. Wincing, he pushed the glass back to the bartender.

"No problem," the bartender said, then proceeded to ready another drink. Placing that one in front of him, he said, "You know where to find me. Just shout for Charlie." Charlie tapped the bar and went off.

Sean felt the warmth in his stomach from the first drink but was still far too coherent for his liking. His thoughts were all about Asher and what they'd done. In some ways, he was glad he hadn't had sex with him. It probably would've made things even more strained than they were now.

How was he going to look at him again? Sean shook his head, throwing back the second drink and indicated to Charlie for another.

He had a little buzz going now which was nice. Sean's thoughts diverted to little Janie. She was so cute —and so clever too. He smiled into his third bourbon; eyes focused on the ice rattling as he swirled it around. He couldn't remember why he thought drinking was a bad idea. It helped to numb him. Maybe this can be his new hobby. He chuffed out a breath, half amusement, half annoyance.

Finishing his drink, he asked the bartender—he had told him his name, but he couldn't remember it now—for another.

When it came to him, he just stared at it. He suddenly remembered what had happened to his parents. What was he doing? He stared at the drink as if it held all the answers. He didn't know what to do about Asher. Sean certainly enjoyed being with him, but he couldn't take it if another person left him. He didn't want to come to rely on someone only to be left alone when the going got tough.

He sipped a little more of his drink but knew he was done.

"Hey, are you doing okay?" The bartender asked, coming back to him again.

Sean gazed up at him and smiled, at least he thought he did. "Yeah, I'm good, thanks. Had a rough day."

"We all get them. Well, I'm heading off, so I'll leave you with Analise now." The bartender—Charlie, he suddenly remembered—thumbed over his shoulder at a pretty blonde woman now behind the bar.

"Thanks, Charlie. I appreciate it." He tried to smile again. "Oh, and I'm Sean."

"Nice to meet you. Enjoy your drink." Charlie walked back over to the other bartender, Analise, and shook his head. Sean smiled to himself. He was probably telling her that he was drunk and not to serve him anymore.

Sean blew out another breath and nursed his drink. He wouldn't drink anymore, but he would still be walking home and fetching his car tomorrow.

His phone beeped, indicating a message had come through, so he pulled it out of his pocket and hesitated when he saw it was from Asher. After opening it, he wished he hadn't.

I'm falling in love with you, just wanted to let you know.

Sean stared at the message with a lump in his throat, his heart beating erratically. Gathering himself, he pocketed his phone and ordered another bourbon. He needed to forget what he'd just read.

After finishing that drink, he stood, bracing himself on the bar until he was sure his legs would hold him. He'd paid his tab, and the bartender knew he was walking home. Sean took a deep breath, then let it out slowly as he made his way—unaided—to the door.

The fresh air roused him a little, but he could tell he was not functioning properly at all, and he shook his head at his behaviour. He couldn't believe he was drunk. He walked down the street slowly, not wanting to go too fast and lose his balance. At the corner, he stepped to the edge, glanced both ways twice and crossed the road. As he got near the other side, he heard car wheels squealing, and a car came barrelling around the corner.

Sean saw its back end spin out, right itself as the traction caught and then fly past him. Unfortunately, it was a little closer than Sean thought, and the car hit him as it went past. He was thrown to the ground, and he shouted in agony as pain flared all through his side and hip.

He lay there for a moment, dazed, and then heard shouting. A man came running towards him with his phone to his ear.

"—please! A man's been hit by a car. Corner of Victoria Avenue. Yes. He's awake, yes. Sir? Can you tell me your name?"

Sean glanced over at the man, realising he'd been talking to him. "Um, Sean." He tried to get off the floor, then groaned in pure agony. His hip was on fire, and even the smallest of movements hurt. He laid back down, trying to minimise the pain.

"Sean? Sir? The ambulance is on its way. It will be here in a few minutes." The man stayed next to him, mumbling, but Sean had checked out of the conversation. He was trying to keep still so he wasn't sick. He didn't know if the nausea was from the alcohol or the pain, but he didn't care. All he wanted was for it to stop.

A few minutes later, the ambulance screeched to a stop next to him, and a paramedic ran to him.

"Sir? Can you hear me?" The paramedic brought his face in front of Sean's, then grimaced slightly.

"Yes." Sean's voice was quiet, and he closed his eyes, hoping to help with the nausea.

"What's your name?"

"Sean."

"That's good, Sean. Can you remember your surname for me?"

"Edwards."

"Good, thanks. My name is Casey. Can you open your eyes for me, please? I need to check your pupils." The paramedic lit his penlight.

Sean opened his eyes but flinched when the light hit them.

"Sorry, once more, please."

Sean opened his eyes again and tried not to flinch this time.

"Thank you. Have you had much to drink tonight, Mr Edwards?" The paramedic was holding a clipboard and writing something down. Sean had to try and remember what he'd asked.

"Um, four bourbons, maybe five. At Crush."

"Okay. Do you normally drink that much?"

"No, never."

"All right. Can you tell me what happened?"

"Um, not really sure. I crossed the road, then heard a car, and I got knocked down." Sean's head was clearing slightly from the cool air, but the pain was still immense. He winced as he tried to move again.

"Okay, Mr Edwards, try and keep still for me." The paramedic shouted to his partner, "I need a neck brace too." Then turned back to Sean. "Okay, what we're going to do is get a neck brace on, just to be safe, then we'll have to move you slightly to get a board underneath you. Once that happens, we'll load you onto the gurney and get you to the hospital to get checked out."

Sean nodded slowly, trying not to move too much. He heard another voice—he assumed the other para- medic—talking to the man that helped him as she brought over the gurney. She passed the neck brace to the first paramedic, and he fitted it in place carefully around Sean's neck.

"Okay, Mr Edwards, I'll be riding in the back with you today. My colleague is called Chloe. We're going to get you onto the board now, okay?"

"Yes. God, this is going to hurt." Sean braced himself for the pain moving would cause him. "Ah!" He blew out a breath loudly, trying not to swear at anyone as they moved him onto his side. He felt the hard board at his back, and then more pain as they lowered him onto it. The paramedics fastened the straps, then they each took an end to lift him up.

"Are you ready, Mr Edwards?" The first one— Casey—said.

"No but go ahead." Sean held his breath as they lifted him, again biting his tongue and scrunching his eyes shut.

He was lowered with a little bump, and then fastened with one more strap.

"Okay, Mr Edwards, we're going to get you into the ambulance now." Casey took one side of him,

Chloe the other, and they wheeled him over to the back of the ambulance. From there, it was several bumps to get him where he needed to be, and the gurney fastened in. Once all that had happened, Sean blew out a breath, hoping he'd be given something for the pain.

"Right now, how much pain are you in, Mr Edwards?" Casey asked.

"A lot." Sean answered with gritted teeth.

"Okay, I will give you some paracetamol for now and then you can chat to the doctor about more when we get to the hospital, okay?" Casey set about fixing him some pain relief. "The police will want to have a word with you too. But they are willing to do so at the hospital." Chloe shut the back doors, locking out the rest of the world.

"Right, here we are. Take these and they should dull the pain a little for you." Casey passed over the pills and picked up his clipboard again. "Can you tell me your next of kin details, please?"

Sean rattled off Max's name and asked Casey to retrieve his phone from his pocket to get the number. Having done so, he went quiet, trying to figure out exactly where the night had gone wrong.

CHAPTER TWELVE

ASHER

Asher was brought out of his sleep by his phone ringing. He moved his hand to the bedside table, blindly reaching for it, then bringing it to his ear.

"'lo?" he mumbled.

"Asher?"

Asher recognised the voice but couldn't place it straight away. He rolled over, studying the screen. *Max.*

"Max?" He glanced over at his clock, seeing it said one a.m. and wondered why he was ringing. "What's going on?" He rubbed his eyes as he yawned.

"I've just got a call from the hospital about Sean. He's been in an accident—he's okay!—but he's hurt."

"Shit! What happened? Why did they call you?" Asher scrambled out of bed, reaching for his joggers and t-shirt from last night.

"I'm his emergency contact—he doesn't have anyone else."

"Sorry. What happened?" He continued to dress as he spoke.

"From what I can gather, he was side-swiped by a car, and he has pain in his hips. I'm on my way to the hospital now. I thought you might want to come."

"Hell, yes." Then he paused. "He might not want me there though."

Max was quiet. "He might say the words, but yu need to listen to what he doesn't say."

"If you think I should be there, then I will. I want to, but I don't want to hurt him." Asher really wanted to go, but he would stay home if Max thought it was for the best. Although if he thought that, then he wouldn't have called.

"Okay, I'll see you there." Max rang off, allowing Asher to collect the rest of his things before running out to his car. He didn't go over the limit to get to the hospital, but he didn't go slow either.

He parked the car, locked it and ran to the accident and emergency area. Max hadn't said where exactly Sean would be, so he thought A&E would be the best try.

Entering the hospital, he found a packed waiting room. He couldn't see Max anywhere.

"Can I help you, sir?" The receptionist stood from her chair, gaining his attention.

"Sorry, yes. I'm looking for Sean Edwards. He was brought in not long ago."

"Can I ask who you are?" she asked.

"His fiancé," Max answered as he walked up next to him. "I know where he is. I'll take him." He directed his last statement to the receptionist with a smile.

She returned the smile with a blush.

After they'd walked further away, Asher said, "Fiancé? What the hell?"

Max smirked. "They wouldn't have let you in to see him otherwise. He's just through here."

Max entered a curtain covered area, and Asher followed, seeing Sean laid up on a bed covered with blankets and a tube sticking out of his arm, presumably for giving him pain meds, or something.

The second thing Asher noticed was the smell. Sean smelled like a distillery. Asher glanced at Max, eyebrows raised in confusion and shock. Sean didn't drink, so why did he smell like he'd bathed in it?

Max caught his gaze and shrugged his shoulders in response.

"Hey, Sean. What'cha doing in here?" Max leaned closer to Sean to get within his field of vision as Sean had a brace on his neck.

"Max?"

"Yeah, it's me. You doing okay?"

Sean blinked his eyes repeatedly as if trying to

come out of a daze. "Yeah, not bad. My hip doesn't hurt too much anymore."

"I should hope not with the painkillers we're pumping into you, Mr Edwards." A doctor entered the area with a clipboard in his hands. "Nice to meet you. I'm just going to take a quick look at your hip and side, and then we're going to get you to x-ray. I want to make sure you haven't broken or fractured anything. All right?"

Sean nodded, wincing.

"We'll wait outside." Max paused and grimaced but ushered Asher out.

"Wait, who's we?" They heard Sean ask as they left, and they glanced at each other, wincing when the doctor answered for them.

"Your fiancé is here, Mr Edwards. You'll be able to see him in just a moment."

Asher and Max waited for Sean to say something, but he stayed surprisingly silent. They heard the doctor talking with Sean, and then moments later, the doctor emerged.

"So, I've taken a look, and he has a huge bruise on his left hip. I don't think it's broken or fractured, but I would still like to get it x-rayed to be safe. I will get someone down here to wheel him up there as soon as I can." With that, the doctor left.

Asher and Max eyed each other again, then Max led the way back to Sean. As they entered, the look

Sean gave Asher broke his heart. Sean stared at him as if he had no emotion whatsoever inside him. He didn't know if it was because he was in pain, if he hated that Asher was there, if it was because he was at a hospital where his parents died, or if the alcohol had numbed him to everything.

He wanted to go over, to take his hand and talk to him, but he knew his reception would be cold. He let Max take control of the conversation.

"So, doctor says you're all bruised up. They'll be taking you for an x-ray soon."

Sean didn't say anything for a moment. "My car is at Crush. Can you see it gets home at some point, please, Max?"

"Sure, of course."

Asher was just about to ask what happened when the doctor popped his head back in. "I'm afraid the x-ray machine is being fixed at the moment, so we're going to be taking you up to a ward for the time being. As soon as it's operational again, you'll be first in line."

At that declaration, Sean closed his eyes. Asher wanted to comfort him, but he didn't think it would be welcome. He glanced at Max, splaying his hands in a "What do I do?" look.

Max indicated to Sean with his head and mouthed, "Say something, jackass." Asher narrowed his eyes at Max then turned to Sean, getting a little closer.

"Sean? How are you doing?"

Sean cleared his throat. "I'm okay." He said nothing else, so Asher tried again.

"What happened? Do you remember?" He stepped closer.

"Got clipped by a car as I was crossing the road." He still had his eyes shut.

Asher chanced touching him and reached for his hand, gripping it gently. Sean flinched but didn't pull away, then after a minute gave a huge sigh and tightened his grip on Asher's hand. Asher closed his eyes in relief, then opened them and peered at Max.

Max smiled and nodded.

SEAN

He hated the fact that he was stuck, lying there unable to move properly. He didn't want to see any sympathetic looks from Max or Asher, so he kept his eyes closed. When Asher had taken his hand, he'd very nearly pulled away, but he felt himself relax more in that moment and decided to go with it. He didn't realise how rigid he'd been holding himself until Asher had held his hand and he'd let go of some tension.

With that relaxation, some of the tension in his head had cleared too. He didn't feel as drunk as he had when he'd left Crush but that could also have something to do with the fluids they'd been pumping into him too. He decided not to say much because he feared what would come out if he did—he already knew he was liable to say too much with Asher around.

He answered questions if he was asked, but he basically just laid there and dozed while Max and Asher chatted around him. He never once let go of Asher's hand though.

Distantly, he heard the curtain move on its track, and he tried to rouse himself a little.

"Mr Edwards, we're going to take you up to the ward now," a kind, female voice told him. "It's not too far, so it won't take long."

Asher began to pull his hand away, but Sean tightened his grip and stared at him. After studying him for a moment, Asher leaned down and whispered, "Let me adjust my grip, okay. It will be more comfortable for you. Then I'll walk next to you as much as I can." Asher kissed his forehead and retreated, letting go for a second, and then was back, linking their fingers tightly.

The nausea Sean had felt when he'd been in the hospital with Asher the first time they'd met, came back with a vengeance when the nurses began wheeling him into the corridor. His grip tightened even more on Asher's hand, and he closed his eyes.

His throat was dry, his heart beat frantically, and his breathing was loud.

"Mr Edwards? Are you okay? Mr Edwards?" A voice came at him, but he couldn't respond.

Asher's hand left his, he had no choice but to let it go. Then a hand threaded through his hair and a face came close enough he could feel the breath on his cheeks. A hand gripped his yet again and he felt it pulled against some fabric. *Asher.*

"Deep breaths for me, sweetheart. Come on, Sean. You can do it. Breathe for me." Asher's voice was the hook he needed to keep himself afloat. Slowly, with Asher's words seeping into his mind, he felt himself calming and coming back to the present.

He took another deep breath, letting it out slowly before opening his eyes to the sight of Asher's big golden-brown eyes fixed on his. This close he could see how long his eyelashes were, the scar he'd never noticed before under his right eye and the mole on his left cheek. These random thoughts kept him grounded.

"That's it, Sean. Good. Keep breathing for me." Asher sighed, the breath flowing over his face in a soft caress. "You scared me there, sweetheart. You need to stop doing that to me." Asher gave a small smile.

Sean realised Asher was stroking his hair and rubbing the back of his hand. He was practically over the top of the bed rails, which couldn't be comfortable, but he was there. When no one else had ever been there for him—at least that Sean had allowed. Asher had just taken control and given Sean what he needed without Sean having realised he needed it.

"Sorry," he croaked out through his dry throat.

"Don't be sorry, sweetheart. You don't need to be. I know how difficult this is for you." A pained look crossed Asher's face. "You're so brave."

Sean felt the stirrings of something he had not seen or felt for a long time. Tears. He didn't want to give in to them, so he blinked them back and sniffed.

He realised then that they were moving. How he didn't notice that before he didn't know, but they were. He stared at Asher again, knowing his eyes were wide with fear, but he couldn't help it.

"It's okay, Sean. We're nearly there, all right. Just hold on to me for a little bit longer." Asher kept his eyes pinned on Sean's, muttering words until the bed began to spin, and then came to a stop. "You did it. We're here." Asher pulled back a little but didn't let go, seeming like he was waiting for Sean to let go first. And he would, as soon as he had the strength to look away.

A few minutes later, he found the courage to study the room he was in, sighing in relief as he found he was the only occupant. With that knowledge, he was able to loosen his hold on Asher's hand, and Asher pulled further away. Taking a deep breath, he finally relinquished Asher's hand altogether.

"Hello, Mr Edwards, nice to meet you. My name is Gloria. I need to get your vitals recorded, and then we will see about getting that brace off your neck, all right?" She didn't seem to require an answer, which was good because Sean didn't think he was capable.

As the nurse busied around takings his obs, Sean started to feel embarrassed about his reaction. He was about to tell Asher and Max they could leave when the nurse saved him.

"Okay, you two. You have five more minutes with him, and then you will have to leave because visiting hours were over long ago and don't start again until the morning." She wrote down in his chart. "So, say your goodbyes. I will be back in five minutes." She gave them a stern look, making Sean smile a little.

They were silent as she walked out of the room, then Max came over. "All right, big guy, I'm heading out. I will nip over tomorrow to see how you are." He rested his hand briefly over Sean's. "Oh, and I'll also ring Clive and let him know what's happened."

"Thanks, Max." He cleared his throat when his voice came out gritty.

"See you later, Asher."

"Bye, Max."

As Max left, Sean almost called him back so he wouldn't have to be alone with Asher.

Asher fidgeted beside him.

"Thank you for your help," he whispered. "But you can go now." Sean sounded harsh even in quiet tones, but he needed to be alone.

Asher sighed. "Okay, I'll go. But I'm coming back tomorrow." Asher held up a hand, stalling Sean's next word. "It's not up for debate." He leaned forward, kissed Sean on the lips before he had chance to protest and walked away. "See you tomorrow, Sean," he called over his shoulder.

CHAPTER THIRTEEN

ASHER

Asher reached home at 6 A.M. ready for sleep, but he knew he wouldn't get any because Martine was dropping Janie off at eight. Any other day, Martine would have kept her until ten or so, but she had a doctor's appointment for her son that day. It wouldn't be fair on her to have to take Janie with her too.

He set about making some coffee, yawning occasionally. He was going to need a huge amount of caffeine to get through this Friday.

As he went about getting some breakfast, he thought about Sean, wondering how often he had panic attacks. He knew what they were because his mum suffered from them, though they were few and far between now because she avoided her triggers as much as she could.

Asher didn't believe Sean had many, but that was two in his company now, granted the first one hadn't been full blown or lasted very long, but still.

He sat drinking his coffee and eating his toast, when his phone beeped to say he had a message.

Don't give up on him. I saw how you were with him, and how he was with you. He may not show it, but he cares for you. I'm going in to see him when visiting starts at ten. I'll let you know what's going on.

Max's message gave him renewed hope he could get through to Sean. He wanted to fight for him, without a doubt, but he also didn't want to push Sean where he wasn't ready to go.

Thanks, I'd appreciate that. I'll have kids with me all day so wouldn't be able to get to him until visiting hours tonight. Hopefully, he'll be out by then.

He hoped for Sean's sake that he was. He wasn't sure how much more Sean could handle.

Standing, he rinsed his plate, refilled his mug and walked into the lounge. He wouldn't sit down because he'd be asleep, but he could at least get the toys and crafts ready for the day ahead. Asher decided to take them for a walk this morning—he could do with the fresh air—and then they could come back here for lunch and play for the afternoon before the school run.

He blew out a breath. It was times like this, he really felt for those people who had little sleep and still had to function the next day.

Martine arrived with Janie a little while later. Asher explained to her what had happened with Sean, and she offered to have Janie again tonight for him. He declined, thinking it would be better if Janie was with him when they went to see Sean, and Janie loved him anyway, so it wasn't a hardship for her.

Asher received a phone call from Max around nine-thirty to say he was on his way to the hospital.

"Sean said he'd had the x-ray, and nothing was broken. He's just really bruised and will be in pain for a few days."

"Thank god."

"I can't believe he was drunk last night. Wasn't he supposed to be at yours?" Max enquired.

Asher smiled briefly. "He had been here. We'd had dinner and movies, and we—" He paused. "Never mind. Anyway, he left here around nine-thirty as if the flames of hell were licking at his heels. I thought he'd gone straight home."

"Obviously not." Max chuckled without humour. "I've not seen him like that since before his parents. He never touched a drop all these years. What happened?"

Asher was silent for a moment before deciding to

go with the truth. "I asked him to spend the night with me. He withdrew and ran."

He heard Max sigh. "Yeah, that would do it. Anything that seemed like it was getting too heavy, would throw him off the train, so to speak."

"Yeah, I figured that's what had happened." Asher rubbed his gritty eyes and stifled a yawn.

"Well I'm nearly there. I'm going to take him back to his house—it's bigger than mine—and try to get some sleep. I'll message you the address, so you can drop by later.

"Okay, thanks Max."

"No problem. Speak to you later." Max hung up.

Asher carried on his day with difficulty. Finally, he said goodbye to the last family and sent a quick message to Max asking him if they were okay to visit.

To be honest, Asher. He's knocked out from the pain meds. I don't think you'd get anything out of him tonight. Why don't you come tomorrow morning instead?

Asher hesitated, then sighed and responded.

I don't want to wait, but okay. I'll be there about ten, is that okay?

Max replied immediately.

Perfect. I'll stay with him tonight so message me if you need to.

Asher's shoulders slumped. He wished he could see Sean and check him over himself—he wasn't a doctor, but that didn't matter. Seeing him with his own eyes would settle his worries. But he could wait.

The next morning, after very little sleep again, Asher shouted for Janie. Last night he'd rung around to find a babysitter, so he didn't have to take her today, but no one was free at short notice. He just hoped Sean would be calmer.

"Hey, sweetheart. We're going to go and see Sean, okay? He's hurt himself, so you have to be careful around him, no jumping on him this time." Asher was careful with what he said because he didn't want to scare her, but he also wanted to make sure she knew not to do her usual jumping on his knee trick.

"Is he going to be okay?" she asked, hugging Albert bunny.

"He's going to be fine. He just has a big bruise. You know, like when you fall over and get the bruises on your legs? He has the same. It's just a really big one on his side."

Janie's eyes were wide, but he knew she understood.

They grabbed their things, and Asher picked up the leftover lasagne from last night to take with them. He wasn't sure if Max could cook, but he thought some home cooked food would be good for Sean—plus he didn't know if he could face eating lasagne any time soon.

Asher set Sean's address into his phone—Max had sent it to him last night—and realised Sean didn't live that far away from him. They arrived within fifteen minutes, mainly due to light traffic, and Janie jumped out bringing her tote bag of toys with her.

He walked up the drive, smiling at the similarities between their houses. From the outside, the houses were almost identical, except Sean's was the opposite way around and had a tree growing up the side of the front door.

He knocked on the door when they arrived, and Max opened it with a smile.

"Hey, guys, come on in." Max moved to the side to let them enter, which Janie did with a bounce in her step.

Asher came in after, allowing Max to take the lasagne from him. "I brought some food in case you hadn't had any or didn't want to cook. Just chuck it in the fridge for now."

"Looks delicious, thanks." Max took it through a doorway, which Asher assumed was the kitchen area. Asher had a chance for a quick look around the hallway, and then Max was back.

"How is he?" Asher asked.

"Quiet. In pain. Sad," Max said with a frown. "I didn't tell him you were coming."

Asher stared at him with raised eyebrows. "Was that a good idea?"

Max shrugged. "Probably not, but forgiveness is sometimes easier than getting permission." He smirked. "Come on, princess, let's go see Sean." Max held his hand out to Janie, which she grabbed without hesitation, and they took off into a room to the left. Following behind, he entered a lounge, stopping just inside as he saw an unexpected sight.

Asher had expected a sleek, minimalistic look with wooden floors and square furniture, maybe a leather sofa. That would have fit the design side of Sean. But what he got was what he could only describe as homely. He was right about the wooden floors, but they had been partially covered by a large soft-looking rug. There was a solid wood coffee table in front of a wood fireplace—perhaps courtesy of Zak—with a large TV above it.

Two other things stood out that Asher wasn't expecting. One was a u-shaped sofa that looked like you would sink into it if you sat on it, covered with several square cushions and throws.

The other thing was the large number of plants that were around the room. Sean had never mentioned a fondness of greenery, but his lounge certainly showed it. Asher wondered briefly whether Max had any input in the interior design of Sean's house.

Sean was sat sideways on the sofa with his legs up,

propped up against some cushions. He had a slight frown on his face that was wiped clean when Janie approached him carefully.

"Uncle Asher said you hurt yourself."

"Yes, I did," Sean replied with a small smile.

"Are you going to be okay?" she asked.

Sean lifted a hand and cupped her cheek, smiling wider at her. "I'm going to be fine. I just have a big bruise that needs to get better."

"Would you like to see my toys?" She sat down and started to get some toys out of her bag.

Max interrupted her. "Janie, why don't we take your toys into the kitchen, and we can have some cookies and milk?"

"Yay!" Janie quickly jumped back up again, causing Sean to flinch and grimace. Then she stopped and glanced at Asher. "Is that okay, Uncle Asher?"

"Yes, sweetheart, that's okay." He smiled at her gently and watched them walk into the kitchen.

Asher peered down to see Sean staring at him, a blank look in his eyes. He approached and crouched down next to Sean. He took Sean's hand and brought it to his mouth, resting it against his lips. He hadn't realised how scared he'd been until he saw Sean again this minute.

"God, I was so afraid when I got the call," he whispered, fighting against tears he knew Sean wouldn't appreciate. Sean didn't pull his hand back, which was a positive sign, but he also didn't say anything.

Asher glanced at him again and saw Sean was staring at the ceiling. He didn't know what else to say. Luckily, he was saved by Janie returning, very slowly and carefully, with a plate of cookies. Proudly placing them on the coffee table, she turned and smiled.

"I brought in the cookies without dropping them, Sean! See!" Janie was so excited, she nearly knocked the plate off with her waving arms.

"Okay! Janie, calm down, sweetheart."

"Sorry. Would you like a cookie, Sean?" she asked politely.

"Sure. Thanks," Sean said, moving to lift himself higher on the sofa.

"Here, let me help." Asher stood quickly to support Sean.

"Thanks," Sean mumbled, not looking at him.

Asher didn't know what to do. Sean wouldn't talk to him. If they'd been alone, he would have made Sean talk, but he couldn't do that with Max and Janie present. He understood that Sean was probably mad at him for asking him to stay last night, but he had wanted him there, and he wasn't going to deny it. Sean seemed to react better when Asher was in control of the situation.

He watched as Janie very carefully passed a cookie to Sean and offered one to Max too. Asher huffed a small laugh when she took one for herself and dropped down onto the carpet at Sean's side, without offering him one.

"Do I not get one?" he said, chuckling.

"Oh, sorry, Uncle Asher." She stood quickly and brought the plate to him.

"Thank you, sweetheart." He sat himself as near to Sean as he could get without touching him. Everyone was quiet while they ate their cookies. Asher kept trying to catch Sean's eye, but he was either staring at his lap, the ceiling or Janie. Asher glanced over at Max, seeing him sat with a frown on his face as he watched Sean.

Max glanced over at him and shrugged.

He decided to leave and let Sean have another day of rest. He had planned to stay for a lot longer, but Sean didn't want him there, that much was obvious. Maybe tomorrow he would be in finer spirits—hopefully, Max could cheer him up.

SEAN

The next day, Sean was hobbling around by himself, even though he was still wincing with every movement. He didn't want to see Asher today. *That's not true and you know it.* He did want to see Asher—and Janie—but he couldn't make up his mind about what to do about everything. His heart and his head couldn't come to an agreement. His heart knew exactly what he wanted. His head, however, would not cooperate and still insisted there was too much of a chance of Asher leaving him. The back and forth he was doing made his head hurt.

"Man, come on, cheer the hell up. You're alive. What more could anyone want?" Max threw himself onto one of the sofas closest to the fireplace. He'd been there constantly for the past two days, except for when he drove home for a bag of clothes. Sean tried to see him being there as an argument against Asher leaving —if Max was still with him, then maybe Asher could do the same—but his brain was having none of it. It was coming up with a million and one reasons why Asher would leave, and he was getting fed up of hearing his own thoughts now.

"They'll be here soon, and you can do some socialising for a change. I'm not the tea maid anymore. If you can walk around? You can make tea." Max chuckled. "I could just see you dressed in a frilly apron."

Sean smiled at the vision. "That's not a very fetching look for me, I don't think."

"I don't know." Max raised his eyebrows whilst inspecting him up and down. "Maybe if there was nothing on underneath and only Asher to see you. It might work." Max laughed as he ducked the cushion Sean threw at him.

Sean let out a groan and held his breath waiting for the pain to settle down.

"You deserved that," Max said.

Sean gaped at him, eyes wide. "What! Why? What did I do?"

"You're being awful to Asher. You hardly said two words to him yesterday; you spoke more to Janie. That's not who you are, Sean. Get your head together, he may not wait forever."

And that there is another reason why I don't want to let him in.

The doorbell rang and Max lifted off the sofa to answer it. Sean knew who it was going to be, and he tried to get in the mindset of having a whirlwind girl and a gorgeous man in his house for the second time in two days. It was more visitors than he'd had in months.

"Sean! Max!" Sean saw Janie run up and jump into Max's arms, flinging her arms around his neck. He thought she looked just like a spider monkey, clinging onto him like that. Sean chuckled at the thought and caught Asher's gaze. He tried to keep the smile, although it dimmed a little.

"Hi," he said.

"Hey, Sean. How are you feeling?" Asher walked slowly forward as if not to spook him.

"A bit better. I can move around a little easier,

probably thanks to meds, too. It hurts when I laugh though." Sean moved himself around on the sofa, so his legs were rested up—it kept some pressure off his hips and side.

"Here, let me help." Asher reached over the back of the sofa to position some cushions behind him. Once he was settled, Asher rested his hand on his shoulder and squeezed gently. Then he let go and tried to rescue Max from Janie's clutches.

"Come on, Janie. Let the poor man go."

Janie reluctantly climbed down and walked around to the sofa. Leaning on the side of it, she gazed over at Sean. "Are you feeling better now?" She rested her head on her arms as she stared at him, so adorable, as if butter wouldn't melt.

"Yeah, I'm feeling better now."

"Yay!" She started dancing around the coffee table, arms wide, swinging her bunny from her fingertips.

"Careful—" Sean heard Asher's warning just as Janie lost her balance and crashed into him. He groaned loudly and curled in on himself. Janie backed away with wide eyes, brimming with tears.

"I'm so sorry, Uncle Sean! I really am! I didn't mean to, Uncle Sean!" Janie began sobbing, and Asher caught her in his arms. Sean stared at Janie, shock ringing through his bones. He frowned, *this was too much, enough now*. His brain was beginning to win this war. He couldn't do this. He couldn't care about this family without it destroying him. So, he wouldn't.

"You need to leave." Sean didn't even realise the words were going to come out of his mouth until they did.

"Sean!" Max's voice rang out in the room.

Asher glanced to Sean in shock. "It was an accident, Sean. She didn't mean to."

Sean softened, and he whispered, "Janie, it's okay, sweetheart. I'm not cross. I'm fine." Janie poked her head out from Asher's chest and stared at him, eyes wet with her tears. He nodded, hoping she understood that he wasn't mad at her. It was the least he could do.

He hardened his heart and stared over at Asher. "I need you to go." Then he got up carefully and walked towards the kitchen. He needed to get away from them. He still couldn't believe what Janie had called him—she probably didn't realise what she'd said, to be fair, she certainly didn't understand why it had hit him so hard. He could only remember how so many people before had left him without anyone at all: his parents, his grandparents—they all left him with nothing. He didn't want to be anyone's uncle.

He meandered over to the kettle and switched it on. He was on autopilot, just going through the motions to distract himself. He didn't know what to do. Well, he did. He was going to do this conversion but keep a professional distance from now on—no more dates, no more late-night visits, nothing. Just work.

Sean heard the front door shut, and he breathed a relieved sigh. He didn't have to face them for a while. Hearing footsteps, he stayed facing the kettle, not wanting Max to start in on him, which he knew he would do.

Sean started when a voice boomed out at him. It was not the voice he had been expecting, and he spun around.

"What the hell do you think you're doing!" Asher's voice rang through the room without mercy. "That girl out there—" he said pointing to the front door, "—is sobbing her heart out again. She thinks you're sending her away because she was naughty." He drew a deep breath. "That's not fair, Sean. You have an issue? You talk to me about it. You don't say things like that in front of her."

Sean could see Asher was steaming, and although he knew Asher was right about Janie, he could feel his temper rising. "I apologise for saying it in front of her. But I'm saying it again now. Leave." He put emphasis on the word this time, brooking no argument.

Asher didn't heed the warning tone though. "No, I'm not leaving because we are having this out once and for all. Why are you running all the time? Why can't you just talk to me?"

"You're smothering me, Asher! You're always

around, or messaging, or ringing. You need to leave me alone. I'm not getting into a relationship with you so you can leave me later. It's not happening." Sean realised he'd said more than he wanted and turned back to the kettle. "Leave."

"No."

Sean swung around, ignoring the pain lancing through his side. "Fucking hell, Asher! I'm telling you now, I'm done. If you want another architect, fine, I'll sort it. But I'm done with you and me. I shouldn't have even started in the first place." He went to storm out of the kitchen, but Asher stood in his way.

"No, no, no. You're not walking away until we've talked about this."

"There is nothing to talk about! For god's sake, Asher. Just leave it alone." Sean heard his voice catch on the last word but hoped Asher hadn't.

"You're making a mistake, Sean. We have so much potential—"

"Enough!" Sean had reached his limit. He knew he was close to breaking point, so he had to get Asher out of here. "I don't want you. I don't want Janie. I don't want a life with you. There. Now leave."

Sean must have stunned Asher into silence because he didn't say a word. He stood and stared at Sean for a few seconds, then he saw as Asher clenched his jaw, nodded briefly and walked away.

Sean slumped against the kitchen doorway as he

watched Asher go, a small place in his heart hoping Asher would turn back around and enclose him in his arms. But Asher went through the front door and shut it behind him. The quiet snick of the lock, sounding like a gunshot in the silence.

Sean slid down the doorframe, and even though it hurt to be in that position, he rested his forehead against his knees, breathing as deeply as he could to clear the lump in his throat.

"You stupid idiot."

Sean glanced up to see Max stood in the hallway, shaking his head, anger etched into his face. "I don't want to hear—"

"You're going to listen. And you need to hear what I'm saying. If you keep pushing him away, you *will* have no one. You will slowly edge every one of us out of your life until you *are* alone. I've come to know you pretty well over the last three years, Sean. I know you can be destructive to your own emotional needs. But this?" Max shook his head again, disbelief shining through. "This? You may have lost the best thing that happened to you." With that, Max turned and walked up the stairs. Sean heard the guest bedroom door shut, and then he was alone. Again. As always.

He closed his eyes, the sound of "Uncle Sean" ringing in his ears. He didn't want to believe anything Max had said, but something was telling Sean that Max had hit it right. Sean was nothing if not determined, and as he manoeuvred himself so he could stand with the least amount of pain, he would not let this break him.

He was happy the way things were. He studiously ignored the pang that went through him with that thought.

CHAPTER FOURTEEN

ASHER

Asher had spent the afternoon consoling, then playing with Janie, trying to undo the harm Sean had caused, however unintentional.

He was in two minds about it all. On one side, he could see that Sean feared people leaving him on his own—Sean inadvertently let that out during their argument. Asher understood that, he'd probably be the same if anything happened to his mum. He didn't have much other family around, just an aunt and uncle, although they didn't have any children. Asher was the last in his line, except for Janie.

On the other side though, Asher was pissed beyond belief. Sean was willing to throw away everything they could have because he was scared. Asher had thought he was stronger than that, but obviously, he was wrong.

He shook his head as he washed up the dishes after dinner.

Janie was in her bedroom, sorting through her cuddly toys. She had told him she was going to find a toy that she could give to Sean to make him happier—her own words. Asher couldn't believe how quickly she had taken to the man, in all honesty. Max, he could understand—he could charm the pants off anyone—but Sean was different, more closed off and distant. He hadn't thought she would take to him as quickly.

But then, Janie had her mother's nurturing personality. Annie had always tried to mend people she saw as needing to be fixed and, nine times out of ten, they were appreciative of it afterwards, even if they had pushed against it at the time.

Asher finished the dishes and wiped the sides, cleaning up ready for the next morning—yet another Monday morning coming around. After the weekend he'd had, he'd be glad to get back to working with the children.

He gazed at the stack of paperwork that needed to be tackled, then at his watch. He'd get to it when Janie was in bed. Either that or he would just go to bed himself and forget all about this day.

Two days later, he was on tenterhooks waiting for Sean to show up to finalise the plans for the conversion. The kids were playing in the garden while he paced the patio. The previous day's phone conversation kept replaying in his head.

He sat down at the craft table with the children and, while they'd played with the glue and glitter, he began his planning for the week. He managed to get two done before his phone rang.

His heart leapt when he saw it was Sean.

"H-Hello?" He cleared his throat when it came out hoarse.

"Hi. I'm just ringing to arrange a suitable time to come around and finalise the plans with you? As soon as this is done, you will be able to contract a builder."

Asher's heart sank. Sean made no mention towards them or the argument the day before—it was all business. Asher pinched the bridge of his nose, trying to stem the tears he knew would easily come. "Um, okay. When do you want to come?" His voice was quiet, he tried not to let emotion into his voice, especially with the children there.

"Would tomorrow be all right? About ten?" There was no indication in Sean's voice that he struggled with the conversation.

"Fine. That's fine."

"Great. I'll see you tomorrow at ten. Bye." And with that Sean hung up.

Asher stared at the tabletop, and he brought the phone down slowly before rubbing his face vigorously. He took a deep breath. If that was how Sean wanted it to be, Asher could do no more than obey. He turned back to his paperwork and tried to get some more done before the school pickup.

After twenty minutes of achieving nothing, he packed it away. He couldn't concentrate enough.

He honestly thought they might have been able to work things out. They could have discussed the argument and tried to get through whatever problems Sean had with the whole situation. After that phone call, he wasn't sure Sean wanted to get through the problems. And Asher was devastated.

When the doorbell rang, Asher rushed around to the side gate and opened it, shouting for him to come around the side. His eyes widened when he saw Max was there too—Sean hadn't mentioned that Max was coming, not that he minded.

"Hey, Max. I wasn't expecting to see you today."

"Hey. I thought I'd bring the plans I'd made for the interior so you can have a look." Max gave him a stare that showed exactly why he was there—Sean had asked him to be.

Sean came in the gate behind Max, walking as fast as his bruised side would allow. Asher could see Sean was tired, his face was drawn, his eyes downcast. Sean didn't look at him, he just brushed past and carried on through to the garden. Janie ran up to Max and jumped into his arms, clinging to his neck as usual. Asher noticed she peeked out to stare at Sean but didn't say or do anything. Sean would struggle to repair their relationship—if he was to continue being in their lives

"Hey, pumpkin. How are you?" Max asked.

"I'm okay. I'm playing with Enrico and Laney. Do you want to come and see?" Janie gave him no choice but to follow when she dragged him off in the direction of the kids. "Enrico! Laney! Come see Max!" Janie shouted across the garden at the top of her lungs.

Asher watched as Max crouched down and shook their hands, smiling and laughing all the while. He wished Sean could be so carefree. He glanced across at him, but Sean was watching the interaction with a look on his face that was either pained or longing, though Asher suspected it was pained because Sean didn't seem to be longing for anything. *Was he bitter? Maybe.*

Asher kept quiet. He wasn't going to make Sean talk if he didn't want to. He was a glutton for punishment, but he'd happily take Sean's silence over his absence any day of the week.

He saw as Max stood and waved to the kids, then walked over to them.

"Sorry about that." He laughed.

"No problem. I know what a tornado that girl can be," Asher said with a smile.

"Shall we look at the designs?" Sean interrupted any further personal conversation.

"Sure." Asher indicated the patio table and chairs

and started over to them. "Do you want any drinks before we start?"

"Nah, I'm good, thanks," replied Max, glancing over at Sean.

"I'm okay, thank you," Sean muttered.

"Okay, then. What do I need to look at?" Asher rested his arms on the table, holding opposite elbows. It was more to keep from reaching out to touch Sean than for any other reason.

Sean fumbled with the folder he'd been carrying and passed it over to Asher. He opened it and took out several pages, leaning back to study them. Every time he saw them, he was amazed by Sean's ability. Not only were there hand-drawn pictures in two-dimensional form, there were also three-dimensional drawings of the garage from the outside at several angles and of the inside. He had also included a couple of digital interpretations as well.

Asher let himself marvel at Sean's ability once more before focusing on what he should be examining. He moved his eyes over the plans, scrutinizing for any reason why they wouldn't work or anything that needed changing, but it all looked spot on.

"They all seem perfect to me. Everything we discussed is there. I'm happy with them." As soon as he said the words, Sean's shoulders seemed to ease a fraction as if he was worried Asher wouldn't like them. Or as if Asher wouldn't *want* them. That was probably more the case; Sean didn't want to lose a potential client.

Asher stuffed the papers back in the folder and slid it across the table to Sean. He turned his attention to Max.

"I come bearing gifts too," Max said as he passed over his folder.

Asher smiled. "I wouldn't expect any less, Max." He opened the folder, staring at what Max had created, blown away a second time. "Wow, Max. These are great." If he thought Sean's had been good, then Max's were just as good, if not better because of the detail involved. He inspected one page, which depicted the floor layout and where certain furniture could be put, then another set of pictures showed a digital three-dimensional take from four different perspectives. Max had also included some fabric swatches, paint colours and ideas for storage, seating and tables.

"This is amazing, thank you. Do you just need me to look through and note anything I don't like, or what?" Asher asked, excited to study in greater detail later.

"Yeah, just have a look through. If you're not happy with any of the colour schemes or fabrics or anything, just let me know and we'll go through to find something more suitable. You have time to decide, after all."

He saw Max glance over at Sean, who had been

silent throughout the whole exchange, then back at him, shrugging in what Asher assumed was apology. Asher shook his head and shrugged back. If Sean didn't want to talk, then that was up to him, but he was not going to sit there and play nice when Sean didn't want to be there.

"Okay, gentleman. Thank you for the designs. Sean, I assume everything can go ahead now?"

Sean nodded, informing Asher that he had been aware of the conversation around him. "I have already filed with Building Regulations for a change of use, and if you agree, the structural engineer will double check the foundations tomorrow morning. If that comes up fine, you are good to go as soon as you've found a builder."

"Tomorrow is fine, get them to call me to sort out a time. And I already have a builder, he can start a week Monday if all goes well."

"Wow, you don't let time pass, do you, Asher?" Max commented with a smile.

"Don't see the point. I wanted it done so I had him on retainer. Hopefully, it will be finished fairly quickly." Asher was pleased he'd decided to shell out the extra money to make sure his builder was available at short notice. Most builders wouldn't do it, but he had offered a good incentive. Brian had been calling on a Thursday of every week to find out whether Asher was ready to go. If he wasn't, Brian filled up his week with bookings, if Asher was, he would start the week after on the Monday. When Asher had the final decision from the structural engineer tomorrow, he'd be able to call Brian and tell him he could start.

"Don't blame you. It will be good to get it finished before the winter comes."

"Definitely, it will make my life a lot easier with the kids."

Max hesitated, again gazing over at Sean, who had begun to watch the kids playing. "Well…" Max stopped and looked over at Asher, shrugging again.

Asher replied, "I guess you guys need to get going." He shook his head at Max's raised eyebrows. He wasn't going to force Sean to interact, especially in front of the kids. Not after what had happened when Janie was there.

"Yeah, okay." Max looked crestfallen. "Give me a bell about those designs."

"Will do. And thanks, both of you. I appreciate what you've done." With that, he walked toward the gate, hearing Max shouting goodbyes behind him. The quicker he got Sean out of there, the better. For them both.

SEAN

Max had not mentioned Asher in any form since they had been at Asher's home two days prior. Sean didn't know if he was happy with that or not. He wanted to know how the designs were coming along, but he also wanted to stay far away from anything relating to Asher.

The structural report had come through clear, so that was now the end of his part of the conversion. He wouldn't need to see him again unless there were any design alterations that needed doing.

Sean was on his way to pick Max up. They had an appointment at Crush to see the manager about an extension. He had been dubious about taking it on to begin with—especially since his last escapade there—but he was intrigued to find out what Tom wanted.

His body had mostly recovered from the 'hit and run' as the police were calling it. He supposed, technically it was because the car didn't stop, but it seemed a waste of police time to investigate it. Regardless, he still had a large yellowing bruise on his hip and side, but it was slowly healing. He could walk without limping or leaning over now, only the occasional twinge inter-rupted him if he bent in the wrong way.

As he arrived at Max's, he went through his phone to check his emails and messages—he knew Max would not be out yet, he was never on time. He'd made a dent in the number of emails he'd received by the time Max climbed into the passenger seat.

"Hello, hello! Are you ready for a fun time?" Max was almost bouncing in his seat.

"What's got you all hyped up?" Sean raised his eyebrows at Max's Tigger-like impression.

"Nothing. I'm just interested in seeing what the manager is wanting. I wouldn't have said the interior needed updating just yet, so maybe it's a different area."

Sean laughed. "Max, did you actually scan the information I gave you?" When Sean, glanced over briefly, he saw Max looking sheepish. Sean rolled his eyes. "Okay, well let me fill you in then. Tom wants to extend into the outdoor area. I don't know exactly what his vision is, but he wants to make the outdoor bit more customer friendly."

Max deflated a little at that. "What do you need me for then?"

"Because he may want to enclose it all. I don't know, that's the thing. You might not be needed, but we'll see when we go in."

By the time they'd arrived, Max had pepped himself up again.

They walked into the bar, heading to the back office where Tom had asked them to go when they arrived. Sean knocked on the office door and waited for the, "Come in," that was shouted from inside.

"Good afternoon, Tom. I'm Sean from Thompson

Architect Company." Sean went towards the desk, offering his hand to shake, which Tom did.

"Ah, Sean. Nice to put a face to a name, although now I've seen you're face I know you're a regular of sorts." Tom turned to Max and offered his hand. "And you must be Max. Sean mentioned you on the phone. And *you* are definitely a regular," Tom said with a twinkle in his eye.

"No point finding somewhere else when you have somewhere you love," Max replied with a smile.

"Well said." Tom moved from behind his desk, walking past them to the door. "Let's go see the area I'm talking about, then you can see what I mean." He walked through the bar to the terrace doors leading outside, exiting and holding the door for them both—it shut with a bang behind them.

Sean walked around as he investigated, noticing the distance from the River Cam. He stood at the end of the grass area and glanced back towards the bar. Tom and Max joined him.

"So, you see what I'm dealing with. No customer wants to come out here. There's no shade when it's hot and no shelter when it's wet."

"It has potential. As it stands now, it's a wasted opportunity. Especially due to the weather we get," he said, chuckling. Sean followed the vines with his eyes up the side of the building and an idea began to build.

"I may have an idea, but I don't really know what you want yet."

Tom waved him off. "Just say what you want." He shrugged. "If I like your ideas, you can have free rein over the design."

Sean peered over at him, eyebrows raised. "Seriously?"

"Yes." Tom nodded in confirmation. "I'm willing to bow down to your knowledge and experience so long as it makes this area useable and, hopefully, bring in more revenue."

Sean nodded. "Okay. Well, while I was at university, I worked on a project for a restaurant that wanted to embrace nature and the outdoors. Their aim was help customers relax and want to spend more time there, equalling more money." Sean looked around again. "I could use the same idea here, although this time you have the actual river as a background, and we can utilise the natural sensory aspects of the area. By that I mean the sounds, the visual stimulation, the smells and textures. Adding in your bar, that includes taste. Then all the five senses are being used within this area." Sean was getting more excited by the minute.

Tom was nodding happily. "That sounds fantastic. But is it possible?"

"Definitely. You could create a, sort of, Garden Bar using a pergola with some trellises. The vines can be woven into the lattice around the sides and the top creating a natural canopy. When it's sunny, it can still get through to keep it warm, but shouldn't allow too much through to make it a sun trap; when it's raining, there could be a retractable roof over the vines—"

Max cut in, "Yeah, I can see that working. If we add some string lights, they can be woven through the grid in the lattice and trellises. It would make it more inviting and soothing. To make it more romantic, you could hang some candle lanterns over the tables." Max was gesturing wildly. "I can see lots of wooden furniture with golds and whites." He hesitated, staring at visions only he could see, then continued, "The deck could be extended. There's plenty of room."

Sean glanced over at Tom, hoping they'd not been completely off base about his vision. Tom, though, seemed entranced. Sean glanced around again. He saw the door, which led to what he assumed was the kitchen. It wouldn't be very appealing to see the employees taking out the trash if you were out here.

The moisture had been a helping hand in developing this nature area. He took in the greenness of the plants. The two old, but thriving weeping willows, whose branches and leaves were grazing the water's edge, were placed on either side of the property. One was near the alley entrance to the rear of the bar; the other in a mirrored position but closer to the decking attached to Tom's office, which he'd seen through the windows when they had been in there.

Sean noted that the outdoor area had a section with a seven-foot brick wall, which would allow privacy from onlookers. As the wind moved the branches, Sean thought he saw a balcony above Tom's office, maybe an upstairs living area. The height of the trees would provide privacy for that area too.

"—an?"

Sean jumped as he heard his name being called in a tone that inferred it wasn't the first time. He looked at Max and Tom, who were observing at him curiously.

"What?" Sean asked.

Max grinned. "Did you hear what we were talking about? Or were you building the area in your head already?"

Sean snorted. "I apologise. What did I miss?"

Max nodded towards the eye-sore of a back door, which looked more like something seen at clubs in alleyways. "I mentioned that something needed to be done with the doors and an extension would work well. Since Tom's focus in the bar is pairing sweet and savoury items with the alcohol that's served, it might be a good idea to create an area where he could sell just the sweet items themselves as well."

"How would that work?" Sean asked.

"An add-on could be built to make a small bakery area, using the walkway as the entry for those who just want bakery items and not the alcohol. Something like a Garden Bar and Bakery?"

Now Max had explained, Sean could see it pretty well. Rubbing his chin, he moved over to see better. "We could create a pergola here too and weave more vines through and over it. It could be a curved version using corrugated polycarbonate so sunlight can get through but no moisture. It could be kept away from the edges slightly to allow the vines to be watered."

Tom nodded; his eyes bright. "I like that. The roofing would probably be better extended all the way to the alley, don't you think?"

Sean smiled. "That wouldn't be an issue. Maybe adding some lattice work to prevent sideways rainfall— a plastic screen that could be lowered, maybe?"

Tom grinned. "I've got the money; you've got the ideas. So far, I like what you've come up with."

Max jumped in. "We should probably find someone local to help with the plants, both the choosing of them and, probably, maintaining them too. A landscaper or horticulturist, or both, would be the best fit, they would be more knowledgeable about the design parameters."

They moved slowly back to the deck area, hashing out a few more ideas.

Tom waved over Sean's shoulder, and he turned to see a guy just about to walk away. "Josh, this is Sean and Max." Tom explained his concept to Josh once he'd joined them, and Sean saw interest in his face.

"If you put some twinkling lights overhead, it would make it more romantic, too," Josh added.

Max nodded, glancing around. "Good idea."

Sean explained some of the thoughts they'd been through, adding, "We can add some potted plants and other vines to enclose the area more. That way, people will feel more sheltered, but the view of the river will still be spread out in front of them. We won't stop anything from blocking that view."

Tom smiled. "Seems like we have a plan, gentlemen. Can you work it all up for me to have a peek at, then I'll speak with the owner?" He gestured them inside.

"Of course," Sean replied. They shook hands. "We'll be in touch." He turned to Josh. "Nice to meet you, Josh."

"Yeah, you too."

Sean and Max made their way back through the bar and exited through the front, heading back to his car.

"Wow. That's going to be some project." Max whistled. "Not sure I can be much help though."

"Yes, you can. You have as much vision about this as I do." Sean hesitated. "But you were right about needing a landscaper or someone. I'll have a look around to see if I can find someone who might be willing to take the job on."

"That's not your job, Sean. You just need to create the designs, not find the people to carry them out."

Sean peered sideways at Max. "Really? I guess you don't want any more business from me then?" he said with a smirk.

Max stopped. "Shit. I never thought of that." He started walking again.

"It would be good to find another contact in this business. I could have fingers in every pie in town by the time I'm thirty!" Sean laughed, clapping Max on the back.

They got in the car. "I am serious though; I will look around and see if someone will do it. It's a big job. It's not just designing and that's it. We're asking them to maintain it as well. It's a big ask for some people."

Max nodded. "Yeah, I can see that. Where are you going to look?"

Sean pulled out into traffic. "Well, obviously I can search the internet for landscapers, but I think I will also ask about in the flower shops and garden centres. They might have a better idea of someone who could do it. And they may know who to avoid."

"Good plan."

Sean, being honest with himself at least, knew exactly why he was searching for a gardener when it wasn't his job. He had been telling the truth when he'd said it would be good for his business to know other people, but that was only part of it. He needed to keep himself busy. Asher was at the forefront of his mind every second of the day. He needed to keep him at bay, and the only way to do that was to surround himself with work.

Finding a gardener will take him a while.

CHAPTER FIFTEEN

ASHER

Asher was ready for another night out when Saturday came—it had been the week from hell. When Sean had left on Tuesday, he'd decided to wipe his hands of the situation. He wasn't going to put Janie, or himself, through it when he knew it was unlikely Sean would reciprocate his feelings.

Asher remembered his relationship with Matt. They had been together for three years, and Asher had been in love with him. He'd thought Matt had loved him too, but unfortunately, not enough for him to stick by Asher when he was granted custody of Janie. It had been okay with Matt when they only saw her two or three times a week, but he didn't want any kids. At least that's what he'd told Asher when he'd left—funny really when that hadn't been the answer Matt had given at the start of their relationship.

He wasn't going to make the same mistake, especially when Janie could get hurt by it this time.

Logan and Trent met him at Crush. They stared at him with wide eyes, so he knew he looked under the weather.

"Okay, let's get some alcohol in you," Logan said, clapping him on the shoulder and guiding him to the bar. "What's your poison?"

Asher blew out a breath. "Just get me a beer for now."

"You sure?"

Asher nodded. He would probably drink something else later, but he just wanted anything for now. He surveyed the room to see who was around.

"Hey, Asher. What's going on? You look like crap." Trent grabbed a beer from the counter before it had the chance to even make a condensation ring and took a huge swallow.

Asher raised his eyebrows and watched Trent nearly finish the whole bottle. "I think I should be asking you that," he said, pointing at Trent's beer. "Thirsty?"

"Trish is giving me hell again. I wish the kids didn't have to listen to her barbs—they're pulling further away every day." Trent shook his head and asked the bartender for another beer.

"What's she been saying now?" Logan asked from Asher's other side.

"Oh, just talking about seeing me around town with other women and how it's not a good impression to give the kids, blah, blah, blah." Trent huffed out a laugh. "The worst of it is, she was making it up. I haven't been out with a woman since Trish left. I don't know why she says all this shit when she knows it's all lies."

"She's trying to discredit you, but for what reason, I don't know," Logan replied. "Keep an eye on the things she says. Make a note even. I don't want this to come back and bite you in the ass."

"How are things with you and Jocelyn?" Asher asked.

Trent shrugged. "Strained, in all honesty. She talks to me like I'm a stranger. I don't know if it's because of what Trish has been saying or if she's just like me." He laughed again. "I used to be quiet and keep to myself when I was her age."

"Really? I never imagined you like that." Asher laughed and took a drink. "And what about Harper?"

Trent looked at the floor. "Not good," he said quietly.

"Oh, there's a booth, let's grab it." Logan had started for it before he'd even finished talking.

Asher and Trent trailed behind, avoiding collisions with other people where possible. He was feeling the alcohol already, and he'd not even finished half, but it was probably because he'd not eaten yet.

After they'd sat down, Asher grabbed the menu. "I'm going to order food. Are you guys having anything?" He studied the menu. He always had fish and chips here, but he fancied changing it up a bit. He saw the lasagne but that brought memories back of Sean and their second date, so he scrapped that idea.

"What's got you frowning?" Logan asked.

Asher blinked up at him. "Nah, nothing. I'm having—"

"Fish and chips!" Trent and Logan said together, laughing.

"—BBQ chicken burger and chips," Asher finished with a smug smile.

Trent and Logan stopped laughing and gaped at him, mouths and eyes wide. Logan was the first to recover.

"What happened?"

"What?" Asher's forehead wrinkled in confusion.

"You only ever order fish and chips from here. So, something must have happened to make you change your usual. So, I say again, what happened?"

Asher blew out a breath and picked at the label on the beer bottle.

"Is it about that guy? The architect?" Trent asked.

Asher nodded slowly. "I'm in love with him."

"Why is that a problem?" Logan seemed confused.

"Because Sean is unable to commit to anyone. He's had issues in his past, and it's making him push me away. Whenever I get close to him, he's okay in the moment, but when his brain engages, it's bye-bye. But I'm done with it now, I can't keep doing this."

Logan whistled, and Trent rested his hand on the back of Asher's neck. "Shit," Trent offered.

"Yeah." Asher proceeded to tell them about the date night with Sean last week, then the accident and how Sean had reacted afterwards. "Janie was inconsolable on the way home. It was as if her favourite star had fallen from the sky." He shook his head.

"I can understand why you need to let go. It's a shame, though. You seem lighter when you're talking about him." Trent smiled a bittersweet smile.

"I don't know what else to do. And I have Janie to think of."

Thankfully, they dropped the subject and gave Asher a reprieve. He didn't have any answers for them anyway, so there was no point discussing it.

"The conversion starts a week on Monday, so that's worked well. I spoke with Brian, and he said everything is set to go ahead."

"Oh, wow, that's good. Did he say how long it would take?" asked Trent.

"He reckons about five weeks maximum, but he thinks he may get it done sooner if they don't come across any problems." Asher was excited about the prospect of finally getting to have a separate work and home life.

They began dissecting Logan's life while they ate their dinner. He'd been alone for as long as Asher had known him—since they were five. Logan was bisexual, but he'd only had one relationship in all that time. Those three years were no longer discussed, but Asher had been glad to see the back of her—not that he'd ever met her. Logan had too much integrity to allow his ex-fiancee's warped views of gay people to affect his relationship with Asher. Logan had plenty of fuck buddies but never for more than a few nights or maybe weeks.

"I'm tired of it," Logan said, sitting back in his seat.

"What do you mean, you're tired? Tired of your job?" Asher mumbled around a mouthful of chips. He was shocked by Logan's words.

"No, no, no. Not of the job. I love being a police officer. But I'm tired of what I see every day. All the shit people put others or themselves through." Logan shook his head. "It gets to you after a while. Depending on what I get called out for, I dread arriving and what I might find."

"And it's bloody long hours!" piped up Trent.

Logan laughed, lightening the mood. "Yes! It's bloody long hours, too."

"Have you met anyone you like?" Asher finished off his chips and wiped his mouth with a napkin.

"Nah, I'm not around enough to make it worth

anyone's while." Logan threw a chip at Trent. "Plus, someone has to keep this guy on the straight and narrow."

"Fuck you," Trent replied, laughing, throwing the chip back. "I don't need looking after."

"Yeah, okay, then." Logan's eyebrows rose at Trent's words.

The rest of the night went by in a similar fashion, all of them getting more and more drunk. When his taxi poured him outside his house at three in the morning, Asher had forgotten all about his problems with Sean.

SEAN

Sean had visited several flower shops and garden centres since the meeting at Crush, and he'd received a couple of recommendations for landscapers who might be able to do such a large project. Unfortunately, when Sean had contacted them, both had said they were booked out for quite a while. He'd asked them to contact him when they had space for the work, but he didn't hold out much hope.

Max dropped by the office to take him out for lunch, and they strode towards the deli.

"Max, hang on," Sean said when he saw a flower

shop on the corner from where they were. He walked towards it and, when he entered, saw it was busy. He waited in the queue with Max muttering behind him, while the assistants dealt with the customers before him.

"—display in my shop. The flowers were beautiful and the way he had arranged them? Absolutely beautiful. He must have hundreds of different types of flowers in that huge house. Where he gets the time to tend to them all, I do not know," one woman said.

"They do look absolutely divine. He has such a way with greenery. It's such a shame he won't come into town more often. He'd have plenty of business if he opened a shop here," the other said.

Sean couldn't keep quiet. "Excuse me. I'm sorry to bother you, but I couldn't help but overhear you talking about someone who grows flowers?"

The two women eyed him up and down. "Yes?"

"You see, I'm an architect and it just so happens I need to find someone who could create a nature area. I've been asking around and so far, haven't had any luck. Would you be willing to give me his details so I could speak to him?"

The woman who had spoken first bit her lip. "I'm not sure…"

"I think it'd be okay, Martha. I'm sure this gentleman wouldn't hurt him," the other woman exclaimed.

"I promise all I want to do is talk to him about whether he would be able to do the job. If he doesn't want to, he doesn't have to." The women seemed very protective of this guy, and Sean was intrigued to know why.

"All right," the one named Martha said, "I will give you his address. But I must ask you to be careful with words around him. He's a very shy and anxious young man and keeps himself away from large crowds."

"They make fun of him, you see," the other woman said.

"Julieta!" Martha scolded.

"Well, they do. I was just trying to warn him that Owen doesn't look like other people. I wasn't being rude." Julieta seemed indignant about Martha's reprimand.

"Well, okay. I'll give you directions," Martha said. Sean pulled out his phone.

He walked out of the shop without speaking to the shop assistants, confident he'd found the person he needed. He headed back towards the car.

"Where are you going?" Max shouted from behind him.

"To see the gardener," Sean called back.

"But what about lunch?"

"We can grab something from the drive through. Come on." Sean picked up his pace. He was excited by the prospect of finally finding someone. It had taken the better part of a week, but hopefully this was it.

They drove out to the edge of Cambridge, almost into the countryside and parked in the small flat area the woman had told them to. As they got out the car, Sean spied the wooden entrance gate she had also mentioned. He pointed at it to show Max, and they started walking. They walked down a quiet lane bracketed by tall brick walls and overhanging trees and hedges. Sean wondered who this Owen guy was. The women made Sean think he would have some physical disability, and people made fun of him because of it.

The lane widened and before them stood a large estate house.

Max whistled, and Sean agreed if he was talking about the size of the place. He walked towards the front of the house, seeing an open door to the greenhouse. He entered quietly, so as not to disturb the guy if he was there, but only saw rows and rows of multi-coloured flowers.

Heading to what he thought was the main door, he knocked. They waited, and Sean knocked again when there was no answer. He was beginning to lose hope that the guy was there but decided he could have a little look around. He exited the greenhouse again and scanned along the side of the house. He was just about to go around towards the back when a voice called to them.

"What are you doing here?" An older man wearing a fraying cardigan walked up to them with his grey Irish Setter following behind.

"We're just here to see Owen about some flowers?" Sean explained.

The gentleman relaxed a little, making Sean even more confused. Everyone seemed to be very protective of this guy.

"Didn't you see the sign?" the gentleman said, pointing to the wooden sign, resting against the greenhouse door.

It showed a large arrow pointing to the right.

"If you read the sign, it will tell you what to do." With that, he ambled off with his dog. Sean turned to read the sign.

If the door is open, but there is no answer, proceed down the path, along the wall to the gate. Then shout, "Gardener."

Sean glanced at Max and shrugged, then walked towards the indicated path. It wasn't a very long path, but it took them around the edge of the property.

"This is weird, Sean. I feel like we're in a horror movie, and someone's going to jump out with a knife," Max said, seriously.

Sean shook his head. "Don't be ridiculous. And you know better than to talk to me about horror movies."

They arrived at the gate and he shouted for the gardener. He couldn't see much of anything except lots of flowers growing up a wall. He watched as Max touched the petals of some of the flowers surrounding them. Sean loved greenery, especially at home, but this was amazing.

He was just starting to get impatient, though, when a young man emerged from behind the wall. Sean couldn't help it. He stared in fascination at the vision before him.

The guy was tall and willowy and was wearing a lavender coloured baggy jumper over the top of what appeared to be a vest top in a similar colour. He also wore a pair of tight, light blue jeans, covered with dirt. But that wasn't what caught Sean's eye the most. The guy, who he assumed was Owen, had the palest skin Sean had ever seen, white-blond waist length hair and bright blue eyes. Sean's first instinct was that he looked like he had albinism, but Sean wasn't one hundred per cent sure.

"Can I help you?" The guy's voice was soft and melodic and immediately put Sean at ease.

Sean cleared his throat. "Sorry, yes. Are you Owen?"

The guy nodded. "I am. How can I help?"

"My name's Sean, this is Max. I'm an architect for Thompson Architect Company. I have a job proposition for you."

Owen studied them both, frowning and biting his lip.

"I heard about you from Martha and Julieta? If that helps?"

After a minute, he moved closer to the gate and reached out a hand to unlock it. As he did, Sean noticed he had long fingers with polished fingernails. Owen let the gate roll backwards for them to enter and stepped out of their way. Locking it behind them, Owen set off around the wall. Sean and Max followed, but both came to a halt when they saw their surroundings.

In every direction, they saw flowers, trees, hedges, vines, bushes and several more greenhouses. The sheer size of the garden area, and what was within it, was impressive—and that was only what they could see. Sean knew then, in his heart, he'd found the person who could do Tom's extension justice. He made a mental note to come back and investigate when he had more time, maybe Owen had some advice about plants for his house.

Owen had carried on walking, seemingly oblivious to the fact they had stopped, so they had to jog to catch up with him. They followed him into a large greenhouse, which was attached to the back of the main house. Owen bent down to a flower, pulling off a small brown leaf, and then turned to them, raising his eyebrows.

Sean fidgeted, then decided to get straight to the point. "I have been asked to redesign an outdoor area at a bar. I have plenty of ideas of how to make it work, but not the knowledge of how to actually create it. That's where, I'm hoping, you come in. The manager is wanting someone who can not only help create the look he wants, but also maintain the area continually."

"How much work is involved?" Owen asked quietly.

Sean and Max detailed the plans they had so far, and Sean saw a light spark within Owen—he hoped that meant Owen would do it.

"Do you think you can do it?" he asked.

Owen surveyed the greenhouse and began wandering, picking at flowers here and there. After a few minutes, he walked back to them.

"Yes. Although I would need to see the area in question first. I do not work well in crowded places, so I would need to see whether it is something I will be able to do."

"I understand. If you let me know when you'd like to take a look, I can make sure I'm there as well."

"Thank you. That would be helpful."

"How did you do all this?" Max said suddenly. "This place is amazing. And huge. Is this all one building?"

"Thank you. And no, there are two separate buildings on the land with adjoining garden areas. They were both family homes that were left to me. I joined them together to create a space of comfort and calm, doing a job I love."

"Does your family live here too?" Sean asked.

"No. I'm afraid they have all passed," Owen said with a sad smile.

Sean swallowed a lump in his throat. "I'm sorry for your loss. I understand completely," he croaked out.

Owen cocked his head to the side and studied Sean. "Yes, I believe you do." He smiled again and turned to tend to some other flowers. "It is easier for me to be here, surrounded by flowers. I feel a connection to them that I have never felt to another living thing. People tend to be…awkward around me. Fearful, even. What they do not understand and all that." Owen turned back to them a neutral look on his face. "Sorry, that was more than you needed to know. I am free Tuesday morning if you would like me to visit the area?"

"That would be great. Do you need me to come and pick you up?" Sean asked, eager to get Owen there now he'd found him.

"No, I shall be fine. I will be there for ten."

"Thank you, Owen, I appreciate it." Sean turned to leave but was stopped by Owen's next words.

"Because of our pasts, we need to learn to embrace our present or our future could be gone within the blink of an eye."

Sean stared at Owen. He felt those words down to his soul; he had no choice. Owen had brought all of Sean's fears to the forefront of his mind, and he realised he feared losing Asher when, in fact, he'd already lost him. He wasn't winning anything by pushing Asher away—he was losing his future.

CHAPTER SIXTEEN

ASHER

Asher had decided to take the children to the park for the morning on the final day of the week. He was still not getting a huge amount of sleep, what between thinking and dreaming about Sean and Janie's nightmares, he wasn't getting a full night *any* night. It was a small consolation that Janie's nightmares weren't every night. She'd had one on Sunday and one last night, so they were coming further apart now. He still hadn't contacted anyone about them, but he would if they continued for much longer.

He smiled as Enrico built a sandcastle, and then Laney flattened it, to which they both laughed and did it all over again. The laughter of the children was a balm to his soul, nothing sounded better.

Janie was climbing along the rope wall with Albert bunny safely tucked in her hoodie. He'd tried to persuade her to leave the bunny with him while she played, but she had adamantly refused. He had learned to pick his battle with her—it was not worth the fight that might have followed.

The sun was shining down on them with a slight breeze bringing a breath of fresh air. This was the time of year Asher loved the best—sunshine and blue skies—it meant they could spend a lot more time outdoors.

Janie came walking over, cuddling Albert bunny, looking wary.

"What's the matter, Janie?" Asher asked, drawing her into the circle of his arms.

"Sean," she whispered so quietly, he strained to hear her.

"What about him, sweetheart?" Asher tried to keep the pain out of his voice.

"He's here." Janie pointed over Asher's shoulder, and he turned his head to look.

They locked eyes for a moment before Janie made her presence known again.

"It's okay, Janie. He won't hurt you."

Janie stared at him frowning. "I know he won't hurt me, Uncle Asher," she said with haughty tone. "He's my friend. I just don't want to hurt him. Like I did last time."

Asher almost burst into tears at that confession. All this time, he thought Janie was scared because of

Sean's outburst, but she was actually scared because she thought she'd hurt him again.

He hugged her close and tried to find his voice. "You won't hurt him, sweetheart. He's all better now. And you didn't mean to hurt him last time either. It was an accident."

"But he asked us to leave?" She looked so confused, understandably.

He could tell a little white lie to help assuage her fears. "It wasn't because you hurt him, Janie. He was really tired and needed his sleep so he could get better."

"Is that why we haven't seen him for a while? Because he was really tired?" Janie gazed at him with hope in her eyes.

He wasn't sure exactly what to say. He didn't yet know why Sean was here, and he hadn't come any closer so far.

"Yes, I think it could be the reason."

"Can I go and see him, Uncle Asher? I want to hug him to make him feel better."

He swallowed to clear the lump in his throat. He was overwhelmed by the size of Janie's heart and the sheer magnitude of her empathy.

"Sure, sweetheart. Just stay where I can see you, okay?" Asher wasn't sure what to say to Sean, so if Janie could break the ice first, it might be easier.

Janie walked around the bench and slowly over to

Sean. When she reached him, Sean crouched down to her height and smiled anxiously at her. Asher couldn't hear what they were saying, but Janie was using her hands to talk as she usually did, and Sean was replying.

Asher glanced at the sandpit to check on Enrico and Laney. She was happily playing in the sand, oblivious, but Enrico was watching Sean and Janie. Asher flipped his gaze back and forth between the three of them until Enrico began to walk towards him.

"Is Sean coming to see us?" he mumbled.

"I'm not sure, Enrico. I've not spoken to him yet." He saw Janie fling her arms around Sean's neck, knocking him on his ass on the grass, laughing.

Sean glanced over at Asher, but he could not decipher the look on his face from the distance between them.

"I'd like to see him again. He was kind to me when I fell over." Enrico sat sideways on the bench so he could still watch.

"He was very kind, yes. Would you like to speak to him?"

Enrico nodded quickly, and although it was likely to break his heart in two, he decided to call Sean over.

"Sean!" Asher waited until Sean glanced at him, then waved him over to join them. He turned back towards the sandpit and kept his gaze on Laney.

"Uncle Asher! Sean's all better!" Asher looked up

and saw Janie was still in Sean's arms and didn't look like she was going to let go any time soon.

"I can see that. Sean, I think Enrico would like to talk to you." Asher nudged Enrico's side when he went a bit shy. "It's okay, Enrico. What did you want to say to him?"

Sean sat down on the other side of the bench next to Enrico, repositioning Janie so she was sitting on his knee.

Laney ambled up to Asher and climbed into his lap, probably not wanting to be left out.

"Thank you for looking after me when I fell over," Enrico said to Sean.

Asher saw Sean's face soften, and he smiled as he reached out a hand to touch Enrico's head. "You're welcome, Enrico."

Enrico moved over to Sean and rested against his side, allowing Sean to wrap his free arm around him. Asher glanced at Laney before the vision of Sean with the two kids made his tears leak out. He took a breath and swallowed hard.

"This is nice." Sean's voice penetrated his thoughts, and he glanced at him, frowning.

"What is?" He looked away again.

"Sitting here in the sunshine with brilliant kids and…an amazing man."

Asher gaped at him in shock. "What?"

Sean smiled softly. "You're an amazing man, Asher.

I should have seen it before. I'm sorry it's taken me so long."

His whispered words had tears threatening again. Asher sniffed and cleared his throat several times before he was able to say anything. "Janie? Why don't you take Enrico and Laney back to sandpit? I need to speak with Sean, please."

"Okay, Uncle Asher." She climbed off Sean's lap, tugging at Enrico's hand. "Come on, Laney. Let's build a sandcastle!"

All three shouted in glee as they jumped back in. Asher watched them for a moment, collecting his thoughts. He was about to speak when Sean beat him to it.

"Do you remember the night of my accident?"

Asher snorted. "How could I forget?"

Sean turned towards him, sitting sideways. "Do you remember sending me a message early that night?"

He frowned, trying to think back a couple of weeks and shook his head. "No?"

"Look at your phone, Asher. Check the messages." Sean spoke calmly as he rested his arm in the back of the bench, not touching Asher but close by.

Asher grabbed his phone out of his pocket and was about to look when he realised what message Sean was talking about. He looked down, blushing.

"You remember?" Sean said with a small chuckle.

He nodded.

"Just so *you* know, I'm in love with you, Asher."

Asher closed his eyes as tears rolled down his cheeks, heart pounding like a drum. He had so wanted to hear Sean say that before, but now he wasn't sure if he could let himself believe it.

Clearing his throat again, Asher asked, "What makes you think that?" He opened his eyes so he could watch the kids playing, trying to keep his emotions in check, though tears still escaped.

Sean blew out a breath, and Asher watched him, seeing Sean's gaze on something in the distance.

"I had a conversation with someone yesterday. They made me realise I was still living in the past, that I had locked my heart away. They said I need to live in the present. I need to build the future I want and fight for it. If I don't want to be left alone, I need to let someone in."

"And you chose me?"

"No." Sean shook his head, his words making Asher turn to him in confusion.

"No? No, what?"

"No. I didn't choose you. I had no choice in the matter. Not one part of me had a choice about falling in love with you." Sean leaned forward, resting his elbows on his knees. "You slipped inside my heart, Asher, and I didn't even realise anyone had the key."

Asher's heart stuttered at the honesty in Sean's voice. But he was scared, he didn't know if he could truly believe Sean…truly believe he wouldn't leave him. He huffed at the thought. Now, he was the one who was scared Sean would leave, instead of the other way around.

SEAN

"Uncle Sean?" Janie ran over to them, and Sean's heart stopped at her words. He expected to feel uneasy like he had the last time she had called him that, but he felt happy.

"Yes, sweetheart." Sean smiled at Janie, waiting to hear what she said.

"Do you want to come back to our house and play?" She was almost bouncing on her toes with excitement.

"I'd love to, Janie, but it's up to Asher." He knew he was playing dirty, but if he could get some more time with Asher, he might be able to help put aside his reservations.

It was strange to be on the other side of the fence now. He knew what he wanted, but Asher was scared he was lying—he could see it in his face. He now knew how Asher had been feeling when Sean had pushed him away.

Sean didn't know why he had accepted everything

so easily, but as soon as Owen had spoken those words to him, he felt freer than he ever had. Everything had clicked into place, and he knew exactly who he wanted to spend his life with—the two people in front of him.

Janie squinted up at Asher, pleading at him with her eyes. He saw the moment Asher relented.

"Sure. Sean can come around for lunch. Grab your things then, kids," Asher called to them. He picked up the backpack he took everywhere with him and double checked a couple of the pockets, probably to distract himself until the kids were ready.

"Are you going straight home?" Sean asked before standing.

Asher peered at him, unknown emotions swirling in his face. He nodded.

"I'll meet you there then." Sean walked with them to Asher's car, and then waved at Janie, telling her he would see her in a few minutes.

As he walked back to his car, his heart was thumping like mad. He didn't think Asher would go somewhere else instead because he wouldn't want to upset Janie like that, but he was scared again. Not because of his previous fear but because he didn't want to lose what had been right in front of him. And there was still a chance he would.

He climbed into his car and rang Max on his handsfree as he drove in the direction of Asher's house.

"Hey, you. What are you doing? Do you want to meet for lunch?" Max's voice came over the speakers.

"No, thanks. I'm on my way to persuade Asher to take a chance on me."

Max was silent for so long, Sean checked to make sure they hadn't lost connection.

"Max?"

"What the hell? Yesterday, you were hell bent on never seeing him again. What changed?"

"You didn't hear what Owen said to me, did you?" Sean had stopped with Owen's words, but Max had kept walking.

"No, and you wouldn't tell me either." Max sounded annoyed by that fact.

"I didn't know what I was thinking at that point, Max. I was confused. I've sorted it out now."

"What did he say to you?"

"Basically, what you've been saying to me for years. But for some reason, his words hit home harder. I'm living for me now, Max, not my parents."

"Woohoo! Yeah!" Max yelled down the line.

Sean grinned, feeling lighter than ever. Then he remembered why he had called in the first place. "He doesn't believe me."

"Who? Asher? Have you been to see him already? I thought you said you were on your way there?"

"I am. But I went to see him at a few places I know he goes with the kids. I found him at the park."

"What did he say?"

"Not a lot. I told him I loved him. I could see in his face he didn't believe me."

"Fuck, Sean. You don't do things by halves, do you?" Max blew out a breath. "You're on your way there now?"

"Yeah. Janie invited me over to play." Sean laughed at that reminder. "Asher was not pleased but couldn't say no to Janie."

Max laughed. "Yeah, I can see why." He was silent for a moment. "What are you going to say?"

"I have no idea. I haven't got anything to give him but what I already have. I don't know what else to tell him. He has every right to not believe me." Sean shook his head, even though Max couldn't see.

"He does, yes. But I know Asher a little now, and I think he'll listen. You just need to be honest. Tell him everything and leave nothing out. That's all you can do. If he turns you away, that's on him, not you."

"When did you get so wise?"

"I've always been this way, Sean, you just never wanted to hear it." Max laughed and hung up.

"Asshole," he said, smiling.

He arrived at Asher's to find his car already in the driveway. He knocked on the front door and waited, hoping Asher would let him in.

It opened, and Asher stood there like a statue.

Sean's shoulders sank, he knew he was fighting a losing battle.

"Do you want me to leave?"

Asher stood there staring at him for a moment. Sean saw him swallow hard, then he spoke with a whisper, "Never."

Sean's heart skipped a beat, and he stepped forward and engulfed Asher in his arms tightly. Asher did the same and nestled his head in Sean's neck. He could feel Asher trembling against him and didn't know if he was crying or laughing. He tried to pull back, but Asher wouldn't let him go. And that was all right with him.

"Uncle Sean? Why is Uncle Asher sad?" Janie walked up slowly, whispering her words.

Asher pulled away, drying his tears—yes, crying—with his hands and turned to look at Janie. He crouched down and held out his arms. She came to him, and he began to whisper to her, too softly for Sean to hear.

All he could see was Janie's face getting happier, then she threw her arms around Asher's neck.

"Yes, please! Really?" She pulled back and looked at him and then, when he nodded, she gazed at Sean. "Are you going to spend more time with us now? Uncle Asher says you are going to be here as much as you can."

Sean studied Asher, seeing a hopeful look on his

face, and he nodded. "Yep, sweetheart. As much as I can."

"Yeah!" Janie jumped around the hallway, and the other two children joined in. Suddenly Janie stopped. "Are you going to be kissing?"

Sean burst out laughing, and Asher blushed bright red, opening and closing his mouth several times. Sean came to his rescue.

"Yes. Is that okay with you?"

Janie was quiet for a moment. "Yes. As long as I get some kisses too."

They both laughed.

CHAPTER SEVENTEEN

ASHER

Two weeks later, Asher, Sean and Janie were having dinner at Romano's, sitting on the patio, enjoying the sunshine with Martine and her family. It had been a lovely get-together, even though Asher had been nervous about Sean meeting Martine for the first time. He hadn't understood why he'd been so hesitant to introduce them—he had made excuses for the last two weeks—but in the end he'd chalked it up to him being worried what Martine would say—with her being so abrupt and all.

He observed the people surrounding him and felt love for every single one of them. Their laughter brought a smile to his face.

He felt an arm slide around his shoulder.

"What are you smiling about?" Sean whispered in his ear.

He turned his head towards Sean, going slightly cross-eyed from how close they were. He laughed and pulled back slightly, splaying his fingers across Sean's cheek, his thumb resting on his bottom lip. As his eyes roamed over the gorgeous face of the man he loved, he still couldn't stop his brain from doubting Sean's intentions, even though Sean had done nothing to disprove them.

"And now you're frowning." Sean reached a hand up and rubbed a finger between Asher's eyes, smoothing the frown away. "So many thoughts in that head of yours."

"I'm smiling because I'm happy. I'm surrounded by people I love, the sun is shining, and it's a Saturday, meaning no work. What more could I ask for?" Asher knew he was avoiding the last question, but he didn't have any answers for Sean on that front yet.

Sean glanced at him, and Asher could see he wanted to ask, but he refrained, probably because of the company. Although saying that, Asher had noticed Sean very often saw things but didn't comment when he easily could have called Asher on his bullshit. Asher was tired of it, so Sean must be too.

Sean leaned forward and pressed a kiss to his lips, then he moved back, peering at him again a small smile in place, those dimples showing very slightly.

"Me too! Me too!" said a big voice coming from a small girl. Janie moved in between them as they laughed. They both leaned down and kissed a cheek each. "Yay!"

As Asher sat back, he caught Martine's questioning look. Asher blushed a little, swearing at his traitorous body. "Janie doesn't want to feel left out, so any time she catches us kissing, she has to have one too."

Martine burst out laughing as did everyone else. Janie just stood between them, looking smug. "I love kisses. And snuggles."

Asher saw Sean bite his lip to keep from responding, whether it was a laugh or a comment he didn't know, but he was glad he kept silent. "Yes, sweetheart, we know you do. Go and finish your dinner now, please."

"But I have finished," Janie whined.

Asher stared at her, and she stopped. "Uncle Asher, I don't want any more dinner, thank you."

He nodded. "That's better. Okay, that's fine. Will you drink your juice then, please, while everyone else finishes?"

"Okay." She skipped back to her seat.

Martine caught his eye. "Do you have her bag and swim stuff?"

Asher nodded and pointed to the floor. "Yes, it's all here." Janie was going for a sleepover at Martine's to allow him and Sean some time alone together. Martine knew he was struggling, so she had told him she was taking Janie and that he needed to talk to Sean about it. He was not looking forward to the discussion, mainly because it wasn't Sean's fault. It was Asher's. And he couldn't help it.

"Great. Well, since we're all finished, we'll head off and leave you two to your evening." Martine winked at Asher, making him blush again.

"Thanks, Martine," Sean said. "It was nice to finally meet you and your family." Sean stood up to shake hands with Ryan, Martine's husband. Martine brushed away his offered hand and pulled him into a hug, whispering into his ear so Asher couldn't hear what was being said. Sean replied, again too quietly, then they pulled away and nodded at each other.

Martine came over to him and pulled him into a hug next. "Don't let your fear get in your way, Asher. Talk to him, get it out in the open, and then you'll feel better about it all. Otherwise, you'll regret it."

Asher nodded into her hair and squeezed his eyes closed, making sure no tears fell. Pulling back, she patted his cheek and leaned down to get Janie's bags.

"Right, sweetheart, are you ready for a sleepover?" Martine asked Janie.

An excited squeal was her answer, and Janie bounced up from her chair and started jumping up and down.

"Janie! Come give me a hug," Asher called.

Janie bounded over and jumped into Asher's arms. He squeezed her tight, reminding her to behave. Then she turned and held her arms out to Sean, who took her from him, and did the same. Then she jumped down and ran to Martine.

"Oh, and we've taken care of the tab," Martine called as they were walking away.

"Thank you!" he called after her, shaking his head. Sean slid his arm around Asher's waist, pulling him close, and they watched as Janie went out of sight.

"Let's go get a drink next door," Sean suggested. Asher nodded and they walked over to Crush, entering the fray. It was quite busy with it being a Saturday night.

Asher was still surprised every time Sean suggested a drink. He still only ever had one drink when they went out, never more, but it was a turnaround from when he refused even a drop. That was another point in Sean's favour—not that he drank, but that he was willing to change his belief about alcohol. Logan had helped him with that, too. He'd explained many times when alcohol had not been involved in a bad situation within his job as a police officer. And that, although alcohol didn't help a situation, it didn't need to be present for there to be a situation in the first place.

Since then, Sean had relaxed his stance and had allowed himself to enjoy a drink, but only if he was not in charge of Janie. Then all bets were off.

Sean and Janie had become close during these last couple of weeks. Sean had kept his promise and was around as much as his job would allow him to be, which was every evening and the occasional times throughout the day in the week. At the weekends, they were together all the time. Janie's nightmares were still happening, but it had reduced to maybe one a week. Asher had told Sean about them, so he wasn't surprised if Janie appeared at any point. He'd asked questions, listened to what Asher had said and offered advice from his own experience.

Sean was opening up a lot about his past, making it easier for Asher to tether the link between his heart and brain. But something was still stopping him from taking the relationship any further.

They grabbed a small table at the back of the bar, and Gemma came over to take their order. As they'd just eaten, they both chose beers.

Asher surveyed the bar, noting people he knew and trying not to feel uncomfortable. He knew he had to open up the conversation but didn't know how to.

"What can I do to help you believe me?" Sean asked.

Asher turned to face Sean in shock. "What?"

Sean gave a small sad smile. "I know you don't believe I'm in this for the long-haul, so how can I help? I'm here, Asher, and I'm not planning on going anywhere. What do I need to do to help you believe that?"

Asher stared at the table and swallowed hard. "I

don't know," he confided. "I just don't know how you can change your mind so quickly, I guess."

Sean blew out a breath, thanking Gemma as she brought the drinks, then took a healthy swallow. "Did I ever tell you the exact words Owen said to me that day?"

Asher shook his head as he gazed at Sean. Sean had told him about his visit to see the gardener and that they'd had a conversation, which had made Sean realise he was wrong about so many things, but he'd never known what was said exactly.

"Owen said, 'Because of our pasts, we need to learn to embrace our present or our future could be gone within the blink of an eye.' I will never forget those words. It made me realise I wasn't living—I was surviving, but that's all. I didn't change my mind quickly, Asher. It may have seemed like it to you because one week I said no, the next I said yes. But my mind had been changing over the entire time I knew you—from the first moment you opened the door of your house." He inspected his bottle, rolling it in his hands. "I kept pushing the feelings down, locking them deep. I didn't want to get hurt, and you had the potential to hurt me the most." Sean met his eyes again. "But I realised with Owen's words, what Max had been trying to tell me all these years. I think I was able to tune Max out because he was always there. Always thought he knew what was best for me. But with

Owen, my guard was down, and his words hit me like a freight train. I realised I would prefer to be hurt if it meant I had the chance to love you and be with you. And Janie, of course," he added with a smile.

Asher wiped at his face, smearing tears. He could see Sean was being truthful, and he felt his reservations begin to drop away. He took a breath. "Let's go home."

SEAN

Sean nodded at Asher's words, relief flowing through his stress-tensed body. He reached for Asher's hand, pulled him to standing and began dragging him to the door. He got waylaid on the way.

"Hey, Sean. How's things?" Tom, the manager of Crush, stood near the bar as they headed towards the exit. He didn't want to be rude, especially as he was technically working for him now, so he stopped to talk even though he was eager to get Asher home.

"Tom! Nice to see you. I'm good, thanks." They shook hands. Tom's eyes flicked to Asher, so he brought him forward to introduce him.

"Tom, this is Asher, my boyf—" He hesitated, peeking at Asher.

Asher smiled at him, then stepped forward, hand outstretched. "Hi, Tom. I'm Asher, Sean's boyfriend."

Sean's heart pounded with the love he felt for this amazing man. "Asher, this is Tom, the manager of Crush."

"Nice to meet you, Asher. I've seen you in here quite a bit with Logan. I'd wondered who'd managed to catch this guy." Tom smiled at them as they stared at him in confusion. He chuckled, then explained to Asher. "When Sean first came here for the job, he looked…empty…for want of a better word. I could see he loved his job, but something was missing. Then he came in the following week with a glow about him. I knew he'd found his happy ever after." Tom smiled at them both again.

Sean blushed, making Asher chuckle. "Yes, I'm very lucky to have caught him." Asher squeezed his hand and wrapped his other hand around his bicep, making Sean blush harder.

Tom laughed. "Well, I'll let you get back to your evening. See you soon." He clapped Sean on the shoulder, turned away and headed towards the other end of the bar.

Sean gazed at Asher, grinned and began dragging him towards the exit again.

It took them the longest half an hour of all time to get to Sean's house. They had an unspoken agreement to go to his house whenever they didn't have Janie with them. A change of scenery. He unlocked the front door and flipped a light on as they entered. Before he could do more than drop his keys into the bowl on the table and slip off his shoes, he was spun around and pushed against the wall. Asher's mouth covered his without fanfare, their bodies melting against each other as their passion began its steady climb.

Asher pressed him against the wall and grabbed his hair in his hands, keeping him steady for the onslaught. Asher nibbled at his lips until he opened on a gasp of much-needed breath, then stroked into his mouth with a talented tongue, mimicking the sexual act he hoped they would get to later. Sean rubbed himself shamelessly against Asher, his arms grabbing tight to the back of his shirt in an effort to get closer.

Sean pulled away to breathe, chest heaving. "Oh, god, Asher."

Asher licked, nibbled and bit his way down his throat, heading further down as he opened the buttons on the shirt. All Sean could do was hold Asher's hair to keep himself steady. Asher moved down his body finally pulling the shirttails from his jeans and pushing the shirt off his shoulders, trapping Sean's arms behind him. Sean's air rushed out, their breathing loud and echoing in the open hallway as Asher attacked his nipples with nips and bites, ramping up his arousal.

"Fu-uck!" Sean struggled to get his arms free, but Asher stopped him by placing his hands against Sean's wrists, pinning them to the wall. Sean struggled as the pleasure became almost too much. Asher lifted his head and pressed his lips to Sean's again, quietening his protests.

"Upstairs! Now!" Asher demanded, letting go of his wrists. Sean was unsteady on his feet, and Asher had to help him up the stairs—or escort him as Asher had hold of the shirt still wrapped around his wrists.

Sean tripped over the steps in an attempt to go faster, and Asher had to steady him several times. He led the way, because, even though Asher knew where his bedroom was, Sean wanted to try and keep a little control. It didn't last long though. As soon as they entered the room, Asher ripped the shirt from his wrists and turned him around, pushing him backwards to the bed. Sean had no choice—and no inclination—to stop him.

"You look so hot, right now," Asher said, voice husky. "All flushed, moaning as if in heat." Asher cocked his head, studying him, and then pushed, making Sean flail until the bed cushioned his fall.

"Shit, Asher, you scared the hell out—" Sean didn't have a chance to finish what he was going to say because Asher had climbed on top of him and silenced him with his mouth. Sean was lost in the sensations flowing through him as he stroked his hands under Asher's shirt and smoothed them over his back. Asher held his head still as he plundered Sean's mouth, making him dig his nails into Asher's back as he struggled for breath.

They pulled apart, their heavy breathing loud in the silence of the house. They stared at each other as they tried to refill their lungs.

Sean stared at Asher. "I love you."

He saw tears fill Asher's eyes. "I love you, too." Sean kissed away the tears that fell and moved his hands to the front of Asher's shirt, undoing the buttons. Once undone, Asher sat up and ripped it off his back then laid down over the top of Sean again, pressing as close as he could.

"Ah!" Sean loved the feeling of Asher's naked chest against his; Asher's subtle chest hair rough against his smoother one, tickling his nipples. Asher began his descent, kissing, licking, nipping his way down Sean's chest to his belt buckle. Observing him from under his eyebrows, Asher undid the clasp and pulled it from the loops, hesitating as he looked at it, then shook his head and put it on the floor.

Sean wondered sparingly what the head shake was for before he lost concentration when Asher opened his jeans roughly, dragging them off his legs with his socks following. Then he was back, smoothing his hands up Sean's legs until he reached his briefs and dragged them down too, making his cock bounce against his stomach. Asher glanced at Sean again with a smirk on his face.

"Oh fuck! Shit! Asher!" Sean shouted as Asher swallowed his cock in one go, no warning except maybe for that smirk. Asher's head bobbed up and down as he worked Sean's cock, leaving a tell-tale wetness behind each time he rose. Sean was so aroused he knew it wouldn't take him long to come like this. "Asher! Stop!"

At his request, Asher's gaze met his, and he slowly licked up his cock before releasing it. "What's wrong?"

"Nothing. I just want you inside me when I come." Sean's eyes widened at the words. He had not bottomed for anyone since college, always preferring the control of being a top. Asher must have seen something on his face because he covered Sean's body with his own and bracketed his head with his hands.

"You okay with that? You don't seem sure." Asher examined his face, concern beginning to replace arousal. And Sean wouldn't have that. He quickly searched his thoughts and decided he was very all right with his announcement.

He nodded. "Yes, I am." He lifted his head to reach Asher's lips and grabbed his ass, squeezing the round globes as he pulled Asher against his arousal. The headiness of being naked while Asher was still wearing jeans was overwhelming.

Sean reached around to undo the buttons, then slid his hands inside, palming Asher's cock over his briefs.

"Fuck!" Asher breathed, his face contorted in pleasure. Asher pumped his hips, nudging Sean's hand with his cock.

Sean slid his other hand around Asher's back and pulled at the jeans, trying to remove them one-handed. "Off!" he demanded when he realised it wouldn't work. He let go of Asher's cock, using both hands to pull the jeans as far as he could. Asher must have realised he couldn't get them off completely because he jumped up from the bed and stripped naked before crawling back up Sean's body.

They kissed slowly, bringing their arousal level higher and higher as they smoothed their hands along naked skin and pressed their cocks against each other. Sean opened his legs, bracketing Asher's hips. They both groaned as the position brought them closer together, their kisses reaching fever pitch until Sean had to break away for breath again.

"Jesus!" he gasped as Asher reached a hand between them and gripped both cocks tightly. Sean bucked and bowed his back, slamming his head back against the bed. He didn't think he was going to survive this. He breathed out in relief and desperation when Asher let go of their cocks and moved to the side. Sean didn't know what he was doing until he placed lube and a condom on the bed beside them. They hadn't been checked yet, so had agreed to wear condoms until they had.

Asher pushed at Sean to move him further up the bed, to which he obliged and spread his legs to make room for Asher. But Asher stayed where he was. He grabbed the lube and spread some over his fingers, spreading some of it against Sean's hole. Without preamble, Asher swallowed Sean's cock again, making him buck up and shout.

"Fuck!" When his body came back down, Asher began his torment. He licked at his cock, flicking his tongue against his nerve bundle and making Sean's head swim, before sucking it into his throat again and repeating. Sean came back to himself when Asher began to penetrate him with a fingertip. It stung a little as it had been a while, but not enough for Sean to stop it. In fact, it felt amazing.

Asher still worked Sean's shaft as his lubed finger pressed and retreated in his ass, spreading him for what was to come. A second finger was added, making Sean wince a little, but a particularly strong suck distracted him enough that Asher could work it in. Asher continued, swallowing him and retreating to flick at his tip before sucking just the head into his mouth. Sean didn't feel any burn in his ass now, even though Asher was still working him.

Asher swallowed him down again as he pressed in a third finger. Sean felt the stretch and burn but was too overwhelmed by the pleasure streaking through his body to care. Sean pushed at Asher's head, letting him know he was close. He didn't want this to end like this. He'd had enough blow jobs off Asher, but he wanted everything this time.

Asher pulled off, lust glowing in his eyes as he surveyed Sean. He reached for the condom, rolling it on before slicking his cock with lube and coming back to rest on extended arms between Sean's legs.

"You okay?" Asher asked, his voice rough from having Sean's cock in it. Sean nodded.

Asher reached between them, grabbing his own cock and positioning it at Sean's ass. Sean widened his legs further, allowing more room. Never taking his eyes from him, Asher pressed forward fighting the resistance until he breached tight muscles. He hesitated once there, checking on Sean again before slowly pressing in and retreating until he was all the way in. Once again, he hesitated.

"Okay?" his voice was strained.

"Fuck, yes! Just fuck me already!" Sean was way past the point of waiting now. He loved the feel of Asher's cock so deep inside of him. "Move!" he demanded.

Asher chuckled and began moving. Pleasure streamed through Sean's body with every stroke, and he grabbed onto Asher's forearms for support. Asher moved one of his arms beneath Sean's leg, opening him up further.

"Fuck me! That's it! Ah!" Asher's speed increased with Sean's words, their naked bodies slapping together.

"Fuck, Sean! You feel so tight!" Asher's head was

bowed as he watched, just as Sean did. The sight of Asher's cock powering inside of his body made Sean's arousal ratchet up further.

"Oh god! I'm not going to last." Sean's grip changed to the bed covers, and he fisted the sheets as pleasure began to tingle in his lower back. "I'm almost there! Fuck, Asher! Come with me!"

Asher groaned, his rhythm faltering for a second before resuming harder than ever. "Fuck, fuck! Come, Sean. Now!"

Sean lost it; the pleasure immense as his body caved to Asher's demand that it let go. His come covered his stomach as he shouted his release, and then Asher's voice joined his. Sean was lost in the feeling of bliss, but immediately wrapped his arms around Asher when those arms failed to keep him upright any longer.

They lay together, breathing heavily against each other's skin. After a minute, Asher moved to grab and dispose of the condom in the bathroom. When he came back, he had a warm cloth which he used to wipe Sean's stomach.

"Wow," Sean said, once they had tangled their limbs together again, Sean resting his head on Asher's chest.

Asher laughed. "Yeah, you could say that."

They were silent for a while, revelling in the post-sex glow. Sean asked something he'd been worried about. "What made you change your mind about believing me?"

Asher didn't speak for a minute. "Your face, mainly. I could see the expressions crossing your face as you gave me your explanation at the bar. And the words you gave me said a lot about how much you have changed your views." Asher kissed his forehead.

"Thank you for trusting in me."

"I do trust you," Asher replied, then explained further. "You're not only taking me on, you're taking Janie on. And I trust you with her. With both of us. With our hearts."

Asher gazed at him, heart in his eyes, and Sean couldn't help it. He leaned forward and sealed the deal with a kiss.

Janie's cry streaked through the air as Sean watched a film in the lounge. He had offered to look after Janie so Asher could go out with Logan and Trent for the evening. He climbed the stairs quickly, heading straight for Janie's room. Opening the door, he saw she was sitting up in bed, clutching Albert bunny.

"What's up, princess?" he asked quietly, kneeling next to her bed.

Janie threw her arms around Sean and climbed onto him, almost knocking him to the floor. He wrapped her in his arms and stroked her hair, gently shushing her. Asher had told him about Janie's nightmares when he first started sleeping over. He'd seen a few now but it had always been Asher who had dealt with it. He was a little lost as to how to deal with it, but he would manage. He would just think about how he would have liked someone to help him when he'd had nightmares after his parents died.

Once Janie had settled into a hiccupping calm, he stood and moved over to her bed. He laid on it, with her next to him and just held her, talking to her gently. Soon, she was asleep, and he rose from the bed. He returned to the film, then he heard a noise and turned slightly, jumping out of his skin when he saw Janie was standing directly behind him. Biting his lip to stop his swearing, he asked her if she was okay.

"Can you stay with me?" she asked timidly.

Sean's heart broke. "Of course, I can, sweetheart. Let's get you into bed, and then I'll lay down with you." He got Janie into bed, wrapped in her covers, and he laid on top—right on the edge of the single bed —resting his arm across her. She put her hand on top of his and snuggled down.

ASHER

Asher returned from Crush to a silent house. It was still early, so he was a little disappointed to realise Sean was already in bed. Then he noticed the TV was still on and went to find him. He was probably in the kitchen, getting a drink or snack.

Entering the kitchen, he saw it was empty, so he placed the dessert he'd picked up in the fridge for later, and he trudged up the stairs to his bedroom. Realising Sean wasn't there either, he tiptoed over to Janie's room. Once inside, his heart grew with love at the vision before him. Janie and Sean were splayed across Janie's bed, limbs in all directions—as much as they could in a single bed—both snoring loudly with their mouths open. Asher held a hand over his mouth to stop his laugh from escaping, he didn't want anything to disturb the precious scene. *I love this man deeply*, he thought as he quietly closed the door behind him.

ASHER

He didn't know what the matter with Sean was, but he was quiet and couldn't seem to concentrate on anything. Asher had seen him bounce from lounge to kitchen to study to lounge for the last two hours. They were heading out to Crush in about an hour, a Christmas party that Tom was holding, but he was concerned that Sean didn't want to go.

"Hey—" Asher stopped when Sean jumped, having apparently not realised he was there. "Everything okay? You seem a little jumpy."

"What? Oh, yeah, I'm okay." Sean's eyes wouldn't meet his, and Asher began to get worried.

"You don't have to come tonight if you don't want to."

"No, no. I do want to come. Everything's fine. I promise." Sean settled and wrapped his arms around

Asher, melting into him. "I'm going to go and have a shower." Sean kissed him on the lips and left the kitchen.

Asher frowned, watching after him as he strode to the stairs. Something was wrong. Asher hoped Sean would either talk to him later or talk to his friends. He traipsed after him slowly.

They both got ready to go out, conversation stilted throughout the process. By the time Jocelyn had arrived to babysit, Asher was inwardly panicking. He knew there was something wrong with Sean but didn't know how to ask him, since he'd already asked once. He decided to speak to his friends and see if they had noticed any difference. He'd bet the answer would be no because even Asher hadn't seen any warning signs before a few hours ago.

Asher was beginning to worry that Sean wanted out. That he was fed up with their relationship. The idea festered inside of Asher for the whole taxi journey to Crush. He didn't know what to do if Sean said he was leaving. It would destroy him—and Janie. Asher found he couldn't look at Sean, he didn't want to see any answers in his face.

They entered Crush to find the party in full swing. Music blared out from speakers hitched to the ceiling, lights twinkled from the disco balls and voices chattered around the room. Asher headed straight to the bar, wanting to get something to drink right from the word go. He was going to need it if the evening went as he thought it would.

The bar was packed, but Charlie was at the helm. Asher held up two fingers to him, and he nodded in answer. Before he knew it, Charlie had deposited the beers in front of him. "I'll open a tab for you!" Charlie shouted to him, then waved as he strode away. He'd gotten to know Charlie a lot over the past year or so, especially as this was their favourite place to come and unwind.

Asher turned and passed a drink to Sean before staring off in the distance. He noticed one of the back doors was open and decided to go and sit in the quiet. At this moment, he didn't care whether Sean followed or not.

Outside in the cold air, he seemed to be able to breathe better. Even though it was freezing, he felt more centred. He glanced around the space seeing fairy lights and candles lit all through the garden, enclosed from the wind by the vines and trees. He wiped a few stray leaves off a chair and sat down, nursing his beer.

He jumped when a hand landed on his shoulder.

"Hey, I wondered where you were. I saw Sean but couldn't see you." Logan's voice was loud in the silence, and probably due to the amount of alcohol he seemed to have imbibed. Looking up at him as Asher was, Logan seemed to sway with the minimal breeze.

"Hi. Yeah, I'm here." Even to his own ears, he didn't sound too thrilled about it.

Logan must have heard the notes too because he asked, "What's wrong? Trouble in paradise?"

Asher winced and didn't answer, just continued to stare out to the river, even though he couldn't see it. He wasn't going to air this issue with anyone, he'd just wait it out. Well, at least until he couldn't take anymore.

Logan nudged his shoulder. "What's wrong?" He sounded more sober now.

"Nothing. I'm fine."

"Yeah, you look it."

"I'm fine," he said more firmly, hoping Logan would get the picture and bugger off.

He didn't. "No, you're not fine. What's wrong? Do you want me to go and get Sean?"

"No!" he shouted, louder than he intended to. "No. Don't get Sean."

Logan was silent for a moment. "I know something's wrong, Asher. Just tell me." His voice was borderline his 'Detective' voice, and Asher knew he had no option. Logan wouldn't let it go and probably *would* go and get Sean.

"I think Sean's going to leave." His voice was so quiet he didn't think Logan would hear. What he didn't expect was for Logan to burst out laughing at him. Asher turned to stare at him. "What the hell? You think this is funny? Fuck you." Asher turned away taking out his fury on his beer bottle by throwing it into the bin too hard, smashing it to pieces.

"Shit, no, sorry. Asher, wait." Logan tried to calm his laughter. "Fuck. Asher, please, just wait here."

Asher glared at him, then nodded, resuming his seat. Logan left Asher and headed back inside. He was gone for a while, and Asher almost went after him. He didn't fancy meeting up with Sean if he did though, so he decided to stay where he was, although he did stand to walk a little closer to the water.

"Don't go too far. The water's closer than you think."

Asher closed his eyes as he heard the voice he desperately didn't—and did—want to hear. "I told Logan I was fine." He didn't turn around.

"He told me. He also said you weren't, no matter what you said," Sean admitted.

"Go back and enjoy the party. I'll be in shortly." Asher blew out a breath, needing to think things through.

"Can you turn around, please?" Sean asked, voice quiet. "I'm getting a bit uncomfortable."

Asher swung around ready to shout at him when his words died in his throat.

Sean was on the ground, on one knee, no coat or anything, shivering. Asher shook his head. "What-?"

"I love you, Asher." Sean seemed to need that to sink in. "I love you." He reached into his pocket and produced a box, which he opened with none of his usual fanfare. Gazing up at Asher, he asked, "Will you marry me?"

Asher's breath caught, and he sank to his knees in front of Sean, tears pouring down his face. He nodded his head, even as he covered his face with his hands. His emotions were all over the place.

"I thought…" he sobbed.

"I know, which is why I had to come and do this now instead of when I had planned to do it," Sean said, wrapping him in his arms. "Somewhere warm," he chuckled.

"Oh, god. Sorry. Let's get you back inside." Asher tried to stand on wobbly legs, but Sean held him tight.

"In a minute. You need to answer my question. Will you marry me?" Sean asked looking him directly in the eye.

"Yes," Asher answered, a huge smile on his face as Sean put the white gold band on his finger.

A loud cheer went up behind Sean and Asher saw what looked like the whole bar, standing by the doors, shouting and cheering for them.

Asher laughed and hugged Sean tightly before lifting them up and walking back towards the bar.

"You do realise you ruined my surprise, don't you?" Sean said snootily.

Asher gawked at him. "What you mean this wasn't surprise enough?" he said, holding up his ring finger.

"No, the other surprise. I had everything planned out. Never mind. We can always pretend this didn't happen and still go through with it."

Asher narrowed his eyes. "We are never pretending this didn't happen."

"Well, at least you saved me from having a panic attack while I carried out my first plan." Sean laughed and holding each other tightly, they strode towards the dance floor for their first dance as an engaged couple.

ONE YEAR LATER

ASHER

Sean had insisted that because he was the one to propose, he should be the one waiting in the 'church' for Asher to appear down the aisle. Asher knew it was also to do with Sean's panic attacks. By already being in the church, there was less attention on him than there would be if he was walking down an aisle. Asher agreed, although he was sure Sean was also milking it for all it was worth.

Asher examined himself in the freestanding mirror that had been placed in Tom's office. He was wearing the usual church attire—a black suit—but it was teamed with a golden-brown button up shirt and bright blue tie. Ginny, Tom's wife, had insisted they wore shirts in the colours of their eyes, her flair for design a godsend in planning this wedding. And Tom was just as amazing, allowing them to have the wedding at

Crush. Asher hadn't been allowed to see the decorations in the Garden Bar area yet, he'd been told it was a surprise.

The door opened behind him, and Logan and Trent came in.

"Ready for your ball and chain?" joked Trent.

Asher smiled. "More than ready." And he was. He wasn't nervous like he'd been expecting to be—he was eager. "Thanks for standing up with me, guys." He couldn't have asked for better friends than these two.

"No problem. That's what friends are for," Logan replied, clapping him on the shoulder.

"Right, we're heading out there to wait. We'll see you in a few minutes. Ginny will come and get you when it's time." Trent pulled him into a hug, then they left.

Asher blew out a breath and checked his appearance in the mirror again. He wanted everything perfect for Sean. His wedding gift hadn't panned out like he'd planned but he wanted everything else to be as it should be. He will just have to tell Sean his gift is delayed. They had started the process to become foster parents three months ago and Asher had spoken with the case worker the previous day, hoping they had been approved in time for the wedding, but the case worker said it was still pending.

Sean had been so excited when Asher had brought up the subject of fostering children. Ever since Sean had moved in two years prior, they'd been talking about children and adopting or arranging for surrogacy—Martine had offered, much to their shock and joy—and then someone had suggested fostering. With the amount of space in the house, they had plenty of room to look after several children, and with Asher's job, the case worker had been more than happy to see them through the process as quickly as possible.

So, Asher understood they were nearly finished in the process, but it was hard having to wait for someone to say they were suitable parents.

Another knock at the door brought him out of his thoughts. Ginny poked her head around the door.

"You ready to go?" she asked

"Yes, please! Get me there already!" he laughed.

Ginny laughed too. "You are eager, I see. Come on, let's go." She opened the door wide, and they headed out.

Asher had seen the inside of Crush when he'd first arrived. The main bar area had been set up with numerous low tables and chairs, having had the bar-height tables and chairs removed for today. The tables had been decorated with a blue tablecloth, white plates and brown centrepiece and napkins; the chairs decorated with white covers and a blue and brown fabric sash. He'd been amazed how much it had changed just because of the decoration.

They walked towards the back doors, which despite

the cool air had been left open. There were heaters spaced throughout the building and outside. He'd been told this when he'd mentioned about guests getting cold.

Asher stood at the doors opening out to the Garden Bar and stared at his future husband. He was aware of Ginny saying something, but he was too busy staring. Around them were all the family and friends that had come to matter the most over the past few years. As the music played and he walked towards Sean, he briefly registered that the lattice work had been draped in sheer white fabric with the fairy lights twinkling above it, giving the light a hazy look. Chairs had been set in rows to create the aisle he was currently walking down.

He cared about nothing at that point except for getting to Sean. Nothing felt more right. He could Sean was staring at him too, hands clenched at his side.

Asher reached Sean, and they immediately clasped hands. If they had been anywhere but here, he would have drawn Sean to him for a kiss, but he knew he had to be patient.

"Are you both ready?" Tom asked. They both nodded.

They had been surprised to find out that Tom could perform their wedding. He had offered to do it but had said they could get someone else if they wanted. Both had agreed for Tom to do it without hesitation, overwhelmed by the sincere gesture.

"First, I'd like to welcome everyone here today to celebrate the union of Asher and Sean. I feel honoured to have been allowed to officiate this marriage and join these two amazing people together in front of the people who matter most to them.

"When two people meet, there is always a journey to be travelled. Some people fall in love straight away and the journey is easy and smooth. For others, the journey from friends to lovers is not so straightforward. I believe that either way, that journey is what brings two people together and is what shows how well you complement each other.

"For Asher and Sean, the road was a little bumpy in the beginning." Some people chuckled at this. "But they reached the other side and, while they are amazing individuals on their own, they became the best versions of themselves together. To be able to love another person more than yourself takes courage, and these two have it in spades.

"To Asher and Sean, family and friends are very important. They care deeply for each other but just as deeply for those around them. And that is why you are all here. So, without further ado, I'll get to it."

Chuckles rang out through the guests, and Asher and Sean joined in.

"Honoured guests, we are gathered here today to

join Asher and Sean in the union of marriage. This contract is not to be entered into lightly but with a realisation of the obligations and responsibilities each has to the other.

"Asher, do you take Sean to be your husband? Do you promise to love, honour, cherish and protect him, forsaking all others and holding onto him forevermore?"

"I do," Asher replied, gazing straight into Sean's clear blue eyes.

"And Sean, do you take Asher to be your husband? Do you promise to love, honour, cherish and protect him, forsaking all others and holding onto him forevermore?"

"I—" Sean coughed to clear his throat, amidst some chuckles. "I do."

"Okay. Asher and Sean will now exchange rings. Asher, please place the ring on Sean's left hand and repeat after me. As a sign of my love, that I have chosen you, above all else, with this ring, I thee wed."

Asher repeated the words as he slid the ring on Sean's finger.

"And Sean, please place the ring on Asher's left hand and repeat after me. As a sign of my love, that I have chosen you, above all else, with this ring, I thee wed."

Sean repeated the words as a tear slid down his cheek, and he placed the ring on Asher's finger.

"And now by the power vested in me, it is my honour and delight to declare Asher and Sean as married. You may now kiss to seal the deal."

Tom had barely got the words out before Asher's lips were on Sean's. Asher tasted Sean's tears as they kissed, and he held him tight. As they pulled apart, he saw Sean's smile was as wide as his own felt.

"Janie?" Tom's voice called out. They turned to watch as Janie walked up towards them. "Janie has something she would like to give you."

Holding hands, they turned to her.

"Uncle Asher, Uncle Sean." She took a breath. "This is a heart from us all to you. A reminder of where you belong." She held out a red heart, the centre embossed with their names. Just like the ones hanging on the noticeboard in the bar.

"A reminder of where we *all* belong," Tom agreed.

"Thank you, sweetheart. Thanks, Tom," Sean said. He saw Asher raise an eyebrow in question, and Sean nodded.

They turned to the guests, seeing the people who meant the most to them—including Darren, Sean's old teacher who he'd finally contacted two years prior. "Thank you for this. We do have one other thing we would like to do today while you are all here," Sean announced.

"Janie, sweetheart." She was wearing a gorgeous white dress with a blue and brown sash and, at nearly eight years old, the necessary jewellery and makeup to match. Asher smiled as she bounced on her toes in front of them.

Both of them crouched down to get to Janie's height, each grabbing one of her hands.

"Janie, we wanted to tell you that the adoption has gone through." Asher waited a moment to see if Janie understood what they were telling her.

Her eyes filled with tears. "Does that mean I'm yours?" she asked quietly.

Asher nodded, tears filling his own as Sean answered. "Yes, Janie. You're our daughter now."

She burst into tears and flung her arms around their necks. Cheers went up from the guests.

Asher and Sean had spoken at length about adopting Janie before approaching her and asking her what she wanted. She had been so excited about becoming their daughter, just as much as they had been. The process had been long, though, and they had almost given up hope. But five days ago, they'd received the news and had decided to wait to tell Janie until today, making it that much more special.

"Can I call you Dad?" Janie asked them both. Tears threatened again as they both nodded. "I love you, Dad," she said to Asher as she kissed his cheek, then turned to Sean. She canted her head before leaning in to kiss his cheek, "I love you, Daddy."

Asher heard her whisper, "I can't call you both Dad."

SEAN

Twelve hours later, they were on the way to their honeymoon—ten days on the Isle of Wight—nothing fancy but special, firstly because it was their honeymoon, and secondly because it was their first getaway alone. They had decided not to go too far in case Janie needed them. She was staying with Martine for the duration.

They had rented a beach house to give them more privacy. Sean doubted they would be going on to the beach much with it being the middle of December, but the views were incredible regardless. He would be just as happy to stay tucked up in the house, cosy with a fire as he would be outdoors. So long as Asher was with him, he didn't care.

An arm slid around his waist as he stared out the window at the view from the house. "You okay?" Asher asked him, bringing a cup of hot chocolate in front of him. He grabbed it and turned his head to the side to kiss Asher's cheek.

"I'm good," he said, taking a sip.

"I know you are." Asher hip checked him as he

chuckled and walked away, making Sean blush in remembrance of the way they had christened the hallway when they'd first arrived. How Asher still made him blush after all this time, he didn't know.

Seven days later, they were lounging on the sofa, wrapped around each other and surrounded by blankets. Asher's phone rang, startling them because it had hardly rung since they'd been here. The only time had been when Janie wanted to talk. The other times, they rang her.

Asher fumbled around to reach it, frowning at the display. "Hello?"

Sean couldn't hear the other side of the conversation, only Asher's responses and facial expressions.

"Hi…That's great news…Okay…Yes…Now?" Asher glanced at Sean, eyebrows raised in surprise. "Can I call you back in five…Okay, thanks…Bye." Asher stared at the phone as he ended the call.

"Everything okay?" Sean reached forward to rest his hand on Asher's arm.

He nodded, then peered over at Sean and cleared his throat. "That was Maggie, the case worker?" Sean nodded he understood. "She says our case has been approved. We can now foster children."

"That's great news. Did she say how long it would

be until a child is likely to be placed with us?" Sean was so excited. He knew he should dial back the enthusiasm a little because if a child needed to be placed with them, then it was for reasons no child should have to go through. But still, it was a huge thing for him. Asher had been reluctant, at first, to choose fostering. His concern was that fostering was usually short term, and he was worried that Sean wouldn't be able to handle the children leaving after a short time. Sean had reassured him that he would be fine, but they could revisit it if it happened.

"That's the thing." Asher glanced up at him. "She has a child who needs a place immediately."

"Right now?" Sean asked.

Asher nodded.

"Then what are we waiting for?" Sean stood up, surveying what needed to be done before they left. He was knocked forward a step when arms banded his waist from behind. "What's that for?" He twisted around to see Asher's face.

"I thought you'd be disappointed about leaving."

"Don't be stupid. I'm more than happy to leave if it means we can help a child."

Asher kissed him but, for a change, kept it brief. Then Asher contacted Maggie, telling her they were on their way home, and they rushed around packing their things, and then packing the car before heading home. They had contacted the rental company, explaining the situation, apologising for leaving the place in a bit of a mess and asked if they could let them know if they'd left anything. Asher had given the company some extra money for their help and understanding.

By the time they'd arrived home, they were both bouncing in their seats. Asher had contacted Maggie again, explaining where they were and when they'd be back; Sean had contacted Janie and explained what was going on.

They'd managed to get their car unpacked by the time Janie had arrived home, thanks to Ryan, Martine's husband, and had checked one of the guest rooms for the child.

Asher hadn't been given much information over the phone, except that the child was a thirteen-year-old boy who had been taken from his parents because of signs of abuse and neglect. It broke Sean's heart to think people did this to others, be it to children or adults.

When the doorbell rang, they all went into the hallway. Asher opened the door to Maggie and a skinny-looking, brown-haired boy.

"Hi, Asher, Sean. I'd like you to meet Maddox."

"Hi, Maddox. Welcome to our home," said Asher softly.

Maddox didn't reply, just glanced at them briefly then around the house. Sean was at a loss, even though they'd been prepared for this situation.

Janie stepped towards Maddox slowly, gripping Albert bunny as usual. She stopped in front of him, garnering his direct attention. Then she reached forward, pushing the bunny against Maddox's chest. In reflex it seemed, he brought his hands up to catch it before it fell.

"Albert bunny will keep you safe. You need him more than I do," Janie said, smiling.

Asher and Sean gaped at each other—Janie had never been separated from her bunny before. They turned back to Maddox, waiting to see his reaction. Sean half expected him to throw it to the floor. But Maddox surprised him.

Maddox stared at the bunny for a few tense minutes—then hugged it tight to his chest. Sean thought he saw tears in the boy's eyes before he looked down. *He* certainly had tears in his own.

ASHER

They strode through the open front door, carrying their precious bundle. Sean had been with her in the back on the way home from the hospital, and now Asher had to chance to hold her again.

Twelve-year old Janie jumped up from the sofa and ran towards them. "Is this her?" she asked excitedly.

"Careful! But yes, Janie, this is her. Let me sit down with her and you can see." Asher sat in the middle of the sofa holding her close, smelling her sweet baby smell.

Sean sat on one side of him, Janie the other. They all watched the tiny baby girl enclosed in a warm blanket.

"What is her name?" Janie asked.

Asher peered at Sean, who cleared his throat. "Patricia."

Janie glanced at Sean. "After Grandma Patricia?" Sean nodded at her. "Oh, it's a lovely name." She jumped up from the sofa. "Maddox! Come here! They're home!"

"I could hear that without you shouting me, pipsqueak." Maddox strode into the room, holding a half-eaten sandwich. At seventeen, he had grown into his frame in the time he'd been with them and, although he still struggled to believe people cared about him, he had agreed that Asher and Sean could adopt him, which they had eighteen months ago.

Asher was sure he would begin to feel more at home, but Maddox continued to keep himself apart from them. Well, Asher and Sean, anyway. Janie had latched onto Maddox the minute he came four years ago and never let go. He often wondered whether Maddox had stayed just because of Janie—she seemed to bring out a little light in him.

"Nice. A baby." Maddox went to stalk away, but Janie had other plans.

"Come here, Mad." She grabbed his hands and pulled him towards baby Patricia. He stood there, unsure, studying Janie, and then the baby, and then Janie again. Asher almost didn't catch the slight softening of Maddox's face, but it was there. It gave Asher hope that Maddox would be okay.

Asher gazed around his family: Sean, Janie,

Maddox and Patricia. Their family had grown, but there was enough love for them all.

Would you like more from Crush? The next in the series is Primary Seduction.

Sign up to my newsletter to get the Crush prequel short story, Love Conquers, and a newsletter serial every month.

If you have a moment, would you write a review for Instant Desire please? Reviews help other readers decide whether they would like to read the book and, therefore, are also important for authors.

ABOUT ELOUISE EAST

I am Elouise East but feel free to call me Elli. I write sweet and steamy connections in gay romance. I also touch on taboo stories under the name Elouise R East.

Books that tell the stories where friendship and family are the focal point - be it blood family or chosen - is very important to me. That's why I include a variety of personalities, talents, ages, situations and abilities as I believe a story needs, or a character needs. I want my characters to be real, to be relatable, to be free to have whatever views they tell me they have. And trust me, most of the time, I do not have *any* say in the matter!

My characters come to life on the page for me as well as my readers. Their stories unfold in front of me, and I have very little input into how they want to be shown. Just like real life, the lives of my characters change with every choice, every interaction and every conversation. And I wouldn't have it any other way.

I write books that are emotionally realistic, even if liberties are taken with other aspects of my stories. I don't know any other way to write. It comes from deep inside.

Who am I? A single parent to two children who make life worth living. An avid reader who still devours every book she can get her hands on. A student of learning about any subject that takes her fancy. An author of books she would read herself. And a romantic at heart who loves anything cheesy.

Who's in?

Stalk me here... ;-)
WEBSITE: https://elouiseeast.com/
NEWSLETTER: https://elouiseeast.com/newsletter
LINKTREE: https://linktr.ee/elouiseeastauthor

BOOKS BY ELOUISE EAST

<u>CRUSH</u>

First Kiss

Instant Desire

Primary Seduction

Deep Down

A Crush for Christmas

Life Support

Covert Strength

Love Scene

Lawful Attraction

<u>JUST A LITTLE CRUSH</u>

Star-Crossed

He's Behind You

A Special Love (newsletter story)

<u>DADDY</u>

Love Me, Daddy

Soothe Me, Daddy

Spoil Me, Daddy

DARK & DIVERGENT

A Biker Make Three

Forbidden Temptation

Too Many Secrets

CHARMED

Treehouse Whispers

Rhythm Inside (Heard it in a Love Song Anthology)